The
Landing

KCP Fiction is an imprint of Kids Can Press.

Kids Can Press acknowledges the financial support of the Government of Ontario, through the Ontario Media Development Corporation's Ontario Book Initiative; the Ontario Arts Council; the Canada Council for the Arts; and the Government of Canada, through the BPIDP, for our publishing activity.

Published in Canada by
Kids Can Press Ltd.
29 Birch Avenue
Toronto, ON M4V 1E2

Published in the U.S. by
Kids Can Press Ltd.
2250 Military Road
Tonawanda, NY 14150

www.kidscanpress.com

Edited by Sheila Barry
Designed by Marie Bartholomew

Main cover image © 2008 Jupiterimages Corporation
Spot image of violin © 2008 Shutterstock Images

Manufactured in Altona, Manitoba, Canada, in 4/2010 by Friesens Corporation

CM 08 0 9 8 7 6 5 4 3 2 1
CM PA 08 0 9 8 7 6 5 4 3

Library and Archives Canada Cataloguing in Publication

Ibbitson, John

The Landing / John Ibbitson.

ISBN 978-1-55453-234-6 (bound). ISBN 978-1-55453-238-4 (pbk.)

I. Title.

PS8567.B34W38 2008   jC813'.54   C2007-906083-8

Kids Can Press is a *l,©rᴜs* ™ Entertainment company

The Landing

A Novel by John Ibbitson

KCP Fiction
An Imprint of Kids Can Press

Also by John Ibbitson:

Fiction

The Night Hazel Came to Town
Jeremy's War 1812
The Big Story
Starcrosser
The Wimp and Easy Money
The Wimp and the Jock
The Wimp
Mayonnaise
Catalyst

Non-fiction

The Polite Revolution: Perfecting the Canadian Dream
Loyal No More: Ontario's Struggle for a Separate Destiny
Promised Land: Inside the Mike Harris Revolution

For Nola, who stayed

Prelude

She had given him a bath, even though it wasn't
Saturday, and dressed him in his best clothes and
pressed down his hair as best she could. His father
had grumbled into his Sunday suit, and she was in
the white dress with the pink and yellow flowers, so
this was something special.

"I don't need to go," his father muttered again,
half-grinning.

"Yes, you do," she repeated, half-grinning back.

"Well, let's go then."

His father was wonderfully tall and terribly strong
and wise in all things, and he took the boy's hand
while his mother opened the back door, which was
the only one they really used, and they stepped into
the cool spring evening.

The sun had set, but only just, with the sky still
light and kids still chasing each other from yard to
yard, as they walked past mostly white-painted
wood-frame houses — though the Timson place was
brick, " 'cause they've made money," as his father had
once explained — and his mother took his other

hand as an old jalopy wheezed past. The boy wanted to take a ride in a car so bad. "Some day," his father had promised, but not yet.

They turned onto the main street, the stores locked and dark, the awnings rolled up, the sidewalks night-empty, until they got to the south end, where they met other people heading toward the Opera House.

The boy didn't know that it was too grand a name for a hall so small, in a town so small, where not a living soul had ever seen an opera, or wanted to. He knew his grandfather had helped build it. "They built it after the town burned," his father had told him the first time he'd been there, "to show we weren't licked." The boy wished his grandfather was alive. He had never known him. He must have been very strong.

"Is it Santa Claus?" the boy asked, suddenly excited, for he had been here once with other children and their parents, and Santa Claus had given him a little toy truck that he still played with.

"No, silly," his mother laughed. "Christmas isn't for a long time."

And he noticed that there weren't many other children as they climbed the creaking stairs.

The hall was bigger even than their church, and the ceiling even higher and the wooden seats even more uncomfortable than church pews. There were two big brass lights — chandeliers, his father had told

him on Santa Claus day — to warm the wooden
walls, and a stage brightly lit at the far end, set up
high so that everybody could see. The hall was
already mostly filled, especially at the back — like
church, again — so they made their way to the front
and edged past the knees till they found three seats
in the middle.

"Now you have to be still and not make any
noise," his mother told him, just like she told him in
church, where she'd press down on his leg if he
squirmed too much — her warning that there would
be no dessert later if he didn't behave, though there
always was.

So maybe it was church in the middle of the
week, which he didn't like the thought of, because
he was getting more church than he needed already,
and he began to feel cross.

But then men started to walk onto the stage, and
they were dressed like nothing he had ever seen
before, in black jackets that were cut off at the front
at their waist but hung down at the back to their
knees, and they had on white bow ties, of all things,
and they carried things with them, and when they
sat down, they began to blow into them and saw on
them and hit them with sticks, making the most
God-wonderful noise, and he grinned and clapped
his hands.

"They're just warming up," his father explained,
which made no sense at all because it was already

quite warm, in fact he wanted to take his jacket off, and guessed his father did, too.

Then they stopped, and everyone fell silent, and the brass chandeliers went dark, and a fat little man walked onto the stage holding a thin little stick, and everybody started clapping, as though he'd done something.

He bowed to the audience, showing the bald spot in the middle of his black curls, and turned his back on everyone and raised the stick and —

Golly!

He had heard music before, of course. Hymns in church, and tunes his father whistled and his mother hummed. But this music washed over and around him, surrounded him, swirled past him, his pulse racing to catch up. All these men, making all this noise, all together, all at once, with this fat little man waving his stick, leading them on. The sound poured into his chest and up and down his spine, dark as chocolate and fast as horses and glorious, glorious. He had no idea what the music was called and neither did his parents and neither did just about anyone else in the crowd. But while the rest of them cocked their heads and listened, smiles of interest and enjoyment fixed or slipping, this boy was drowning, gasping, coming up for air, diving back in, wanting to drown.

His father looked down at him and nodded to his

mother, who looked down as well. He was leaning forward, breath frozen, his eyes unblinking, his hands clenching his knee.

"Like it?" his father asked, but the boy didn't hear, heard only the music accelerating, growing louder still, unbearable, making him want to yell back at it, until it smashed to a stop, leaving only an echo in the sudden silence.

People applauded, but the boy didn't applaud. He clambered onto his seat, his eyes locked on the stage, trying to see, but he couldn't see because the people in front had stood up, still clapping, and he looked at his father in desperation, and his father laughed and grabbed him around the waist and hoisted him into the air until he was taller than anyone in the crowd.

The fat little man was bowing again, and all the other men were standing, holding their instruments, smiling and nodding. The boy wanted to touch them, wanted to be with them, wanted to know their magic more than he had ever wanted anything.

The conductor noticed him, this boy in the fourth row being held in the air by his father. Their eyes met. The boy stopped breathing, forgot even his father, held out his arms, beseeching.

The conductor smiled, and bowed to him. A private bow, a private smile. A salute. *Welcome.*

And then he straightened quickly, nodded to his players and left the stage, and left the boy amazed.

The Haircut

D, E, F-sharp, G, A —

"Damn."

The A sounded sick. More like A-flat, or A-squished. It was the tuning peg. It just wouldn't hold the tension in the A string anymore. Ben gave it a quick half-turn and tried again. Becky cackled her complaint.

Ben didn't enjoy practicing in the toolshed any more than Becky enjoyed sitting through endless scales on a beat-up violin that wouldn't stay in tune. But Becky didn't have a choice, and neither did Ben. The other hens had taken a dislike to Becky, and so she had been moved to the toolshed to keep peace. Henry hated the sound of the violin, wouldn't have it in the house. The toolshed was twenty yards from the house, though, and Henry's bedroom was on the other side, facing the lake, so if Ben got up early enough, he could squeeze in among the rakes and shovels and hoes and baskets and milk canisters — and Becky — and practice for an hour in the stuffy, heating air until Henry was ready for breakfast, when he would yell,

"Enough!"

Ben slipped the fiddle into a battered and cracked wooden case, grabbed a basket and collected Becky's egg, which had arrived with the squished A. Then he ducked into the henhouse, where other hens chirped and squawked as he took their eggs from them.

"Morning, Olivia. Morning, Sally. Morning, Elizabeth ..." The fact that Ben's mother gave the hens names drove Henry to swearing. But she was fond of the hens and named them, and that's all there was to it.

Six this morning, not bad. There'd be a few more before noon. Some lucky cottager would buy the surplus. The cottagers were always asking if there were fresh eggs for sale.

But Celia wasn't laying anymore; she'd be stew soon. Ben didn't like it when a hen became stew, though he liked the stew well enough.

"Ben, where are the eggs?"

"Coming."

She was in the summer kitchen, which was really just an extra stove out on the screened porch where breezes swept away the heat. On a hot day like this, the stove in the kitchen could turn the house into a sweatbox.

"Thanks, son." She smiled at him. There had been a time when that smile was the most important thing in his life, his only anchor, but he was fifteen now, and he had other things on his mind. She smiled at him anyway, whenever she saw him, even though he never smiled back anymore.

Ben's mom began cracking eggs sharply into a cast-iron pan where the bacon was already spitting, while Ben ran upstairs to his bedroom, shoved the violin under the bed and tucked in the sheets. He hadn't slept well — it was only late June, but a July heat hung over everything, and he had struggled through the humid night thinking about the violin, about whether he was getting anywhere with it, about how to find enough money for a better one. He knew there wasn't enough money; there never would be, though that didn't help him get to sleep.

The smell of the bacon got him back downstairs and into the kitchen, where Henry was already bent over the table, staring at his coffee. Ben poured himself a cup, adding a bit of milk from the icebox, even though Henry thought everyone should drink their coffee black, because he did. Ben didn't know if he put milk in his coffee because he liked it or because Henry didn't.

"You didn't set the table."

"I know." Ben gulped a mouthful of coffee and then grabbed the knives and forks. Though you'd think Henry could do it himself, just once.

Most people called Henry Hank, but Ben's mother didn't, and Ben didn't. The day they moved in, Ben had called him Uncle Henry, but he just scowled. "Henry's good enough for me."

That was six years ago, after his father died, after Mom moved back to her old home, where her

brother Henry was the only one left because the
others had all gone to their reward or Saskatchewan.
Henry never smiled, never had a good word. He
seemed to resent everything in his life — the half a
farm they farmed, the half a life they lived, Ben's
violin, Ben. Henry and Ben were pretty much at war
now, the two of them, though they rarely spoke
and never raised their voices. The war was fought in
the silences.

"Ben," his mother called.

He walked quickly out to the summer kitchen,
where three plates were heaped with eggs and bacon
and toast. It was the same every morning, except
when there was no bacon — it cost money to fatten
up a pig — but the eggs had just been laid, and
Henry had butchered and cured the pig himself, and
his mom had made the bread. It was fine.

Balancing the three plates, Ben walked carefully
back to the kitchen while his mom poured hot
water into the pan to let it soak. She joined them at
the table, and they ate silently, as always. Then they
waited, as always, until Henry was ready to declare
Ben's agenda: "Need you to weed the patch this
morning." "Need you to clean out the barn." "Want
you to take some supplies over to the Weismillers."

They had twenty acres of hay and oats and
turnips, all for the six cows, which gave milk that his
mother churned into butter. There were a dozen
hens, and a pig sometimes, and on the one patch of

decent earth they grew vegetables for themselves and sold whatever they could spare.

But mostly they had a dock, which is why their place was known as Cook's Landing, and why cottagers would roar up in their boats for gas and whatever milk or eggs or butter there was for sale. Henry bought the gas from the company in town, sold it to the cottagers and tried to make a living off the markup.

It had never been much. But since the Depression hit, it was even less. A lot of the cottages had closed up, people didn't use their boats as much, and credit was hard to get in town. They kept themselves fed and paid their taxes, at least the ones they had to.

For once it was his mom, not Henry, who broke the morning's silence.

"Jed's sobered up. I want Ben to get a haircut."

In town, which was forty minutes away by boat — at least their boat — everyone seemed to take either to religion or drink. That's all that was left after the pioneers discovered their farms were good for nothing but pine trees and rocks. So there was the doctor who was always on the bottle and the doctor who was always quoting the Bible at you. There was the drunk dentist and the Baptist dentist. There was Claude, and there was Jed.

They owned a barbershop, where most of the time it was just Claude, a thin, pinched, sour little man who shaved every man's head to within an inch of its life, leaving women to wince and vow they'd do it themselves next time. Jed, however, was a sculptor, who could subdue the unruliest mop and make a farmer look like a matinee idol, at least for a day, and whose sad gentleness made him scorned by some and pitied by others, because most of the time he was soused.

Jed never tried to cut hair when he was on a bender. He just took to his little, white-painted house out on the Jones Road and pulled the curtains and stayed in there for as many days or weeks as it took for him to work through whatever it was he worked through.

And then one day he'd reappear at his chair, beside the glowering Claude, and women would hurry their men to him, while there was still time.

"He doesn't need a haircut, Mary," Henry scowled, as he concentrated on sopping up the egg yolk with his toast.

"Yes, he does," his mother replied firmly. Ben knew she would win. On almost everything, Mary deferred to Henry, because this was his farm, and he had let her come back, and it wasn't worth it to fight constantly with such a man. She only stood her ground on things that mattered — like letting Ben practice his violin, or making them all go to church on Sunday, except in the summer, and, today, having Jed cut her son's hair.

"He can take the launch and pick up a bag of flour and some tea and — well, I've made a list."

"I can see Ambrose." Ben was sitting straight,

watching the two of them attentively. Ambrose Heidman had taught Ben everything Ben hadn't taught himself about the violin, and a chance to stop by and practice with him for an hour was gold.

"No, you can't," Henry snapped. "There's too much to do on the island."

Ben glowered and slumped. A trip into town, and no lesson. It wasn't fair. Though Ben was painfully aware of how much there was to do on the island.

The message had come just two weeks ago. Someone had bought Pine Island. It was only a five-minute row from the Landing, an oblong strip of granite about a quarter mile from end to end, covered in white pine, mostly, though there was birch and maple, too, with a fine old cottage smack in the middle, mostly hidden by the trees. At least it had been fine when the Carlsons owned it, before the Crash, when they'd stopped coming and everyone knew the place was for sale, though no one wanted to buy.

But someone finally had — Americans, apparently, from New York — and they were arriving sometime around Dominion Day. They wanted the place fixed up and had wired up cash in advance. But there was a lot to fix, and most days Henry was too busy pumping gas or working on engines or caulking other people's leaky boats to go over. So he'd left Ben to do it himself, and though Ben was strong for fifteen — wiry, his mother said, though Henry just called it skinny — the work left him drained at the end of the day. Henry had helped him patch the roof where it was leaking and replace the cracked panes of glass, but everything inside he'd done himself, cleaning out the mouse dirt, scrubbing the floors, washing the walls, which were lined in cedar, washing the windows with water and vinegar, scouring the stove, laying in wood for the stove and the fireplace — worst of all, getting the bird's nest out of the chimney and scraping off the soot, which left him so filthy it took three swims and lye soap to get him clean.

And that was just the basics. The cottage needed to be painted, but he hadn't even started taking off the old paint yet, so the place looked like sin, and rotten planks on the front porch were a menace. There were things that needed fixing that he knew he didn't even know about yet. So, yes, there was lots to do on the island.

They finished breakfast in silence, until Henry shoved himself away from the table and limped outside, on his way to the dock. Ben sometimes wondered whether it hurt Henry to walk. Maybe that's what made him always on the edge of losing his temper. Henry was already shorter than Ben, who was still growing, and he was so thin that you could count his ribs when sweat stuck a shirt to them, and his skin was darkened and roughened by sun and work, but it was the limp that defined him. It was really a lot more than a limp, though Ben didn't have a proper word for it. With each step, he threw his right leg forward, swinging it around in an arc, transferring his weight to it while advancing his good left leg, and then he did it all again. He had fallen under a thresher when he was a child, and there was no money for a doctor. The bones had never set properly, and he hadn't walked right since and had never married. Who would marry a man crippled like that?

Ben went to help with the dishes, but his mother shooed him out of the kitchen, because she wanted him on his way. The list was long: a fifty-pound sack of flour, kerosene for the lamps, lye soap, lard, tea, salt, that sort of thing. She took the money out of a battered old cash box that she kept in the pantry and counted out the dollars.

"There, that should be enough. But get your hair cut first." She ran a playful hand through the thicket that he never tried to comb, making him duck away. "Lord knows, you need it."

He headed to the barn, where his mom had already milked the cows and let them out to graze, picked up a straw hat he'd left there and then loped down the broad slope to the dock and hopped into the launch. It had probably been a fine boat, twenty years ago, but now the engine belched and the mahogany had been painted over and everything was worn and chipped and frayed. It had seen half a dozen owners before Henry finally took it off a cottager's hands in exchange for fixing up a boathouse, and Henry was probably the only man on the lake who could keep it dry and running. They tied a scow to the side for big jobs like hauling dirt or wood, but even without the scow it was the slowest boat on the lake — or seemed like it to Ben. But it could get you to the Narrows in twenty minutes and to town twenty minutes after that.

Henry was on the dock, spreading whitewash around the planks with a broad brush, because Mary insisted everything had to look just so for the tourists. Ben knew Henry was watching him, disapproving, as he got behind the wheel. A deep breath, a silent prayer, and he turned the key. The starter groaned, the engine coughed, and died. He let out the choke a bit more and tried again, but the motor just sputtered, and now there was sweat trickling down his neck. Henry started to get up with a "let me do it" grunt, but Ben turned the key one last time, and the motor caught. He pushed in the choke and revved the engine.

"Don't hang around in town. There's too much to do."

"I won't."

And he slipped the lines, edged the boat away from the dock and was on his way.

A string of islands, rock rising from water, fringed with birch and crowned with pine, each standing a couple hundred yards offshore, ran down the west side of the lake, forming a sort of channel that protected boats from the open water, which could get very unpleasant very quickly if your boat was small or, more likely, you were a cottager who didn't know what you were doing. The launch could handle anything the lake could throw at it, but the channel was still the shortest route to the Narrows, so Ben pointed the boat south, perched himself on the back of the cracked leather seat and tried not to think too much.

Thinking was driving him crazy these days. It was all he did now, and it was mostly misery. He would think, as he tried not to think now, about how hard life was in Henry's shadow, how no one understood that he couldn't spend forever pumping gas on a dock or tending a failing farm. "You can get a trade," Henry had told him once during a rare, out-loud argument about what Ben was going to do with himself. "You could apprentice as a carpenter, maybe." But Ben didn't want a trade. His hands didn't understand wood the way his father's had. His dad had been a fine carpenter, a craftsman; the china cupboard in the kitchen was his, and people said you couldn't have gotten anything finer if you'd ordered it from Eaton's. Ben wasn't his father's son when it came to driving a nail, or his uncle's nephew, for that matter, when it came to fixing a balky motor or welding two pieces of broken metal into one.

Besides, Ben had a trade. It was the violin.

Because he had begged, his parents had saved their money and started him on piano lessons when he was only five. But they didn't have a piano themselves, couldn't afford it yet, and one day the furniture store on the main street brought in a violin and a guitar, with books on how to learn to play. His dad had bought him the violin and the book that went with it, which proved useless. But Ambrose Heidman lived in town, and he was a fine fiddler — went down to Toronto once and played in a square dance competition, and the only reason he didn't win was because it was fixed, everybody said — and he gave Ben lessons for twenty-five cents a week, and then, after the funeral, he gave them for free whenever Ben could get into town or he could get out to the Landing, "because that boy can play like nobody's business," he'd told Ben's mother.

Ambrose was a happy man, with no hair but lots of gut and a huge laugh and nimble fingers, and it was fun to be around him and a joy to play with him, because he knew all the things Ben didn't know, like how to get your fingers around a certain scale or how to make the violin play two notes at once. Ben would have practiced with him every day and certainly needed to see him every week, but it was more like once a month, if they were lucky. They'd spend an hour or two together, and Ben would show Ambrose what problems he was having, and Ambrose would show him the fingering to fix it, though last time they were together he'd shaken his head. "I don't know how you do that. I've never even tried it."

And at the end they'd pick up their fiddles and play some tunes, because Ambrose Heidman's great gift was his ear — he could hear a tune once and play it and could improvise freely on anything, and there was a lilt to his playing that meant you just had to dance another one, even if it was late.

"You got it, too," Ambrose had told Ben, and in the last year they'd played at a couple of weddings together and a couple of dances, and people said they were so good together you couldn't hear better on the radio. Ben had brought home a dollar after the first gig and given it to Henry, who'd shoved it in the cash box without a word, as though he resented the money. Ben burned with anger, and the next time he put the dollar in the cash box himself, in front of Henry, making a show of it. He and Henry spoke even less to each other after that.

Most days, though, Ben played alone, practicing the studies, etudes they were called, in the books that Ambrose had given him — "I'm too old for practicing, anyway. You might as well have them" — and playing and replaying his prized pieces of sheet music: "Who Is Sylvia?" "Long, Long Ago," "Shall We Gather at the River?" and his favorite, "Air on a G String," by J.S. Bach, which was so sad and so beautiful, "and that's real music, let me tell you,"

Ambrose had agreed. He practiced in the morning until Henry made him stop, and he practiced if he could get free of his chores and Henry was away, and he practiced at dusk sometimes, until the dying light and Henry's protests — "Will you quit that infernal noise?" — forced him to give up. He wished he had a hundred songs, a thousand, to play and practice, but all his mother could afford was three or four at Christmas, when sheet music was the only present Ben asked for.

He squinted his eyes against the sun. It was hot, and not even ten, and the first trickle of sweat dribbled down his back beneath his shirt. But when he came to a gap in the islands, a gust of breeze from the open water beyond freshened the air. His thoughts turned back, against his will to what he was going to do, if anything, after the summer. He knew his mother was worried about it, too, but "maybe something will turn up" was the most she could think of, with a helpless shrug. He wanted to play the violin. That's all he wanted to do. That's all he wanted to be. But there weren't enough weddings and dances in the district to provide more than pocket money, an extra dollar for the pot now and then. He had to think of something else or life would become the Landing, forever. But what? He wished, as he still wished every day, with a dull ache, that his dad were alive.

His father had been up in the bush with a logging crew near Algonquin Park, where a lot of the local men went in the winter because there was nothing else. He was leading a team of horses pulling a sled of pine logs through the bush. But it was muddy and slippery, and the logging road was too close to a bank that led down to a creek, and the bank gave way, and by the time they got the logs and the sled off him it was too late, though they saved the horses.

"When we lost Jake Mercer, we lost the best we had," one of his father's friends had said at the funeral, as Ben sat in the pew staring at nothing, holding his mother's cold, trembling hand. Muskoka was a beautiful place, the tourists said, and on a warm summer's day, when the blue lake glinted in the morning sun, framed by granite and pine, Ben knew what they meant, understood why they traveled so far to stay there and never wanted to leave. But part of him hated the place. It had killed his father. He spat into the lake and turned the wheel, swinging the boat to starboard.

He had reached the Narrows. The lake ended here, except for a narrow channel barely wide enough for the steamers that plied the lakes — delivering passengers and provisions and mail to the islands and resorts — to squeeze through. There was a tiny lighthouse at the entrance that Isaac Barnes looked after for a hundred dollars a year, guiding boats and ships that had stayed out after dark, because without the lighthouse the Narrows would be impossible to find. It could be tricky to navigate if the wind was fresh from the west and the water was choppy, but not today, and Ben steered the scow between the rocks and trees that lined each side of the shore until he passed into Muskoka Bay, which was really another lake, though a smaller one.

What little breeze there was left him when he left the lake. The bay was dead calm; sweat dampened his shirt; sun burned his forehead. To heck with it. He idled the motor, kicked off his sneakers, shucked his clothes and knifed into the water.

The familiar shock of cold slapped his skin, then dissolved as he thrust himself forward underwater, enjoying the coolness, the freshness of it, surfacing twenty feet from the boat. A quick check to make sure it wasn't drifting, and he began to swim, a forward crawl, almost silent as he sliced cleanly through the waveless surface. He'd been swimming since he'd been talking, as his mother joked, and he could crawl across the quiet lake for an hour, back and forth, hypnotizing himself with his own rhythms, feeling the water course against his pale skin, which never properly tanned, propelling himself with his feet, pulling himself forward as his arms reached out and drew away, stroke, stroke, stroke.

But there were things to do. He circled the boat, one broad ring, then a narrower one, then out of the water and onto the boat, and one quick dive back in, a sprint out and back, and he pulled himself out of the water and slid on his pants, dipping his shirt in the bay before putting it back on. It would be dry again by the time he reached town.

The town was Gravenhurst, twenty minutes later, at the end of the bay, a ghost bay of failure and fore-closure. Ben scanned the empty sheds of the Mickle sawmill that dominated the western shore. A year earlier lumber had screamed beneath its saws, gray smoke had belched from its stack and drifted across the bay, hovering over the great piles of sawdust that lined the shore. But the clear cuts had stripped the district of timber, and the hard times had stripped away business, and the mill had closed the year before. To the east, near Muskoka Wharf, the freshly bankrupt Ditchburn boatworks sat idle; everywhere along the shoreline sheds sat empty, uncared-for, defeated.

Muskoka Wharf, however, was still the town's pride, wide enough to host a station and train tracks for the Muskoka Express, which steamed north from Toronto every weekend — every day it had been, sometimes, before the Depression hit — emptying its carloads of vacationers, who promptly walked all of ten steps to where a steamer was waiting to glide them up the lake to their cottages or resorts. There was no train this morning, and only one steamer idled at her moorings: the *Cherokee*, white-painted, gray-hulled, sleekest and most beautifully propor-tioned of all the ships of the Muskoka Navigation Company. They were beautiful on the water, ambling lazily between the islands, black smoke drifting from their stacks, decorated with passengers in carefully chosen outfits of this-old-thing corduroy and cotton. But bad times were bad for the steamers, too. It didn't help that the government had paved the road as far as the town to give men work, and there were plans to keep the road going up the west side of the lake to Bala. "These boats won't be around much longer," the captain of the *Islander* had warned Henry last summer. The *Islander* steamed empty past the Landing most days, delivering little but mail.

On a busy weekend, the wharf would still be crammed with people and boats, and it could take forever to find a space to squeeze into. But on this Monday morning, with no train today, there was hardly anyone about, and Ben eased the launch alongside and quickly jumped out to secure the bow and stern lines. He'd have to wheedle the Passmores into helping him bring down the supplies, because the main street was almost a mile from the bay, and the flour alone would be more than he could carry. But first the haircut, his mother had said. Passmore's would always be there, but who knew how long Jed would stay on the job.

There was a decent hill, rising from the bay to the main street at its crest. The road leading up from the bay was lined with elms, maples and oaks, guarding broad lawns and substantial homes with verandas and bay windows, houses of brick, or white paint and black trim, with everything kept just so. The homes had been built by mill owners, mostly, in the days when Muskoka Bay was lined with sawmills, and logs choked and fouled the water. Now the town doctor and the owners of the better stores lived there — though even here, Ben noticed as he walked gratefully beneath the shading trees, the paint was peeling on a couple of houses, and everything wasn't just so anymore.

"Gravenhurst Barbers," announced the painted sign on the grimy window, where a row of green spikes in pots — mother-in-law's tongue they were called, and a barbershop was a good place for gossipy plants — hid the interior from view.

Ben stepped inside and searched for a chair. Three men in work clothes, caps or straw hats still guarding their hair, slouched patiently, waiting their turn. Silent, tanned and creased faces stared at knees, and everyone was hot, because the slow-turning fan overhead did nothing, really, to stir the air. The place was crowded, and the wait would be long. But they would wait. They had been ordered to wait.

Ben slipped into the only available chair, the one closest to Claude. No wonder everyone avoided him, and avoided looking at him, with his beak for a nose and claws for hands and the disorderly wisps hanging from his scalp, a poor advertisement for his services. He shot Ben an expectant, hopeful look, but sank back into his own chair at the "Thanks, I'll wait" shake of Ben's head. They were all waiting for Jed to finish with Gideon Smalley.

Gideon was shorter than most men, and richer than most men in town. He boasted the smooth skin and confident good humor of someone who had made a success of himself, and he smiled in satisfaction as Jed the barber clipped and snipped and sculpted his pompadour of snow-white hair. Gideon owned the good restaurant in town and had a phenomenal memory, so that if he met you once when you visited Smalley's Dining Room, where the blueberry pie was talked about in two provinces and three states, he would remember you again, even if it was years until your next visit. Gideon Smalley's perpetual smile, his amazing memory and his business smarts had made him rich and made him mayor, three terms in a row, and earned him and his gentle, nervous wife the right to sit in their own pew in the Presbyterian church, which was the largest in town. And only Jed, of course, could touch Gideon's hair.

Jed's eyes were the saddest thing Ben had ever seen — large, brown eyes framed by the bags beneath them and the gray brows above them. Only his apologetic smile could lighten them. No one knew what it was that made Jed so sad, because he always smiled, and his voice was as soft as cat's fur as he clipped away, comforting, reassuring, wanting no one to have a care in the world as long as they were in that chair.

"Now the Leafs, I think they can go all the way,

Mr. Smalley, I really do." Jed's voice floated through the room, his scissors hovering in one hand, comb framing the next batch of hair to be cropped in the other. "Red Horner's got a lot of heart, and there isn't a better forward in the league than Charlie Conacher. You don't want it too short, now, do you?"

"Whatever you think is best, Jed. You're in charge," Gideon purred back. "But I don't know about the Leafs. They always break my heart."

"Oh, I never give up hope, Mr. Smalley, never," Jed replied. "Shall we do same as last time?"

"Certainly, Jed."

Jed took a wooden tube from the shelf and drew out several long, wooden matches.

"Now don't set me on fire, Jed," Smalley chuckled.

"No danger of that, Mr. Smalley," Jed replied as he lit the match. He combed a swatch of hair away from the scalp, then quickly lit the hair with the match and as quickly snuffed out the spark between his fingers, leaving the hair blackened and singed. Ben jerked back in astonishment, and the other men looked hardly less surprised, but Gideon just smiled into the mirror, and Jed murmured on, about the Leafs and the heat and the town and its troubles — "but we're going to turn the corner soon, I just know it, we'll be turning that corner soon" — and as he moved his hands along, touching the flame to the hair, snuffing it out, repeat, repeat, the blackened tips seemed to give an added sheen to Gideon Smalley's mane, making it even sleeker and smoother, reminding everyone else in the room that Jed was an artist and Smalley was a success and what were they?

Ben didn't know, but for the moment didn't care, sitting in that heat-stifled room with those men, as dust wafted in from the street and Jed sculpted Gideon Smalley's hair with flame and grace, while Claude glowered and the fan carved uselessly through the thick, sticky early summer air.

Ruth Chapman

Ben stared glumly down at the rotting planks of the dock, wondering whether he was going to get an earful. From the defiant frown Henry had worn all day, Ben guessed that his uncle was thinking the same thing.

They were waiting for the new owners of Pine Island to arrive, to inspect the work that they'd done. Only they hadn't done nearly enough. They had tried — Ben had been working morning till night seven days a week on the place, and Henry had come over whenever he had an hour free, which was almost never. But the place had run down, and they hadn't even begun to run it back up again.

Take the dock they were standing on. The foundation was sound enough: the Boyd brothers had laid the cribs — stones encased in squared pine logs that would withstand half a century of shifting ice; and the broad beams underlying the dock had only been laid in the twenties and were good for another decade at least. But the overlying planks had been exposed to too much sun and too much rain, and some of them were rotting and some were cracked, just like the planks on the front porch. They should all have been replaced, but there hadn't been time. There hadn't been time for a lot of things.

The house was dry, at least, thanks to Henry showing Ben how to shingle a roof, though there'd been a lot of swearing and "Sorry" before he'd got the hang of it. There was half a cord of wood stacked along the north wall for the stove and the fireplace — though there hadn't been a night that needed a fire since the end of May — and everything was clean. Ben had oiled the hardwood floors and fixed the sag in the icehouse and brought in enough ice, and covered it with enough sawdust, to last the rest of the summer. But he still hadn't stripped the old paint, let alone laid down any new; three of the shutters needed fixing, and so did the floorboards in the pantry. The door to the root cellar at the side of the house where the milk and vegetables were kept cool was threatening to fall in.

Would they get someone else to finish the job? Would they demand their money back? Ben frowned, and Henry scowled, and they waited.

The settlers who came to the district in the 1860s and 1870s — the Mercers and the Schultzes and the Barneses and the Schells and the Clipshams and the Boyds and the Harbridges and the Heidmans and the two or three dozen other families who had opened the Muskoka District — had lived with failure and loss from the start. They had been promised free land and, yes, the land was free, but the land broke their backs. They cleared the trees — sold them off, if they could, burned them if they couldn't — and dug out the rocks that littered the thin, sandy soil, and planted their first crops. But the rocks came back the next year, a mystery and a curse, until the settlers realized the frost was heaving more rocks up from the deeper earth with each thaw. Without the trees to anchor it, the soil washed away. There were patches of clay where indifferent crops could be grown, and Cook's Landing was like that, which is why they still farmed it three generations after the first refugee from the Old Country had staked the claim. But no one got rich farming in Muskoka, and few were anything but poor, and most gave up and left after selling their waterfronts to the industrialists from Pittsburgh and the bankers from Toronto who had just discovered these pristine waters.

So it was the cottagers now who owned the lakes. The locals made what living they could from selling whatever the cottagers needed, or just wanted. The sons of pioneers planted flowers in the cottagers' window boxes, and took the high and mighty to fishing holes and then cooked them their catch, and fixed their boats and replaced their propellers — because the rich are a menace on the water — and made as much money as they could pry from their guests until the guests went south with the first frost, leaving the locals to survive as best they could through the long snows until the tourists came back.

Most of the Muskoka-born just shrugged at the way things were because what could you do? But it gnawed at some of them; it ate away at Henry like beetles in a tree. He worked the farm that had twisted his bones, and skinned his knuckles loosening seized bolts on misfiring engines, and listened silently while the owner complained about the bill and demanded ten percent off — and got it, because both sides knew he could go somewhere else next time. Henry would watch, his face a mask, as the man took out his fat wallet and peeled off a couple of twos.

A few of them were nice, in that "And how are you today?" tone of voice, and a few tried to be chummy and told their friends "that fellow who fixed my boat is a good man," though everyone knew who was the better man. Some of them treated the locals like dirt. Last year a fat face over a bloated belly had pulled up to the dock and yelled to Ben, "Boy! Do you sell smokes?" Ben would never forget that as long as he lived.

So who knew what the new owners would say when they found that their house in the woods wasn't all pretty like they wanted. "This is egregious," a cottager had once complained when Ben had planted the geraniums too close together, as though Ben knew what "egregious" meant, when everyone in Muskoka finished school in grade eight because that's all there was, except for the merchants' sons who went on to the high school in town. Would the new owner think Ben's work was egregious, too?

He looked across the water to the Landing. The dock, the flat rock that formed the shoreline rising gently to the little plateau, the trim white house, two stories, the barn in back, the shambly henhouse, the toolshed, the outhouse, the vegetable garden behind, then the back field, all framed by bush, starting to fill back in now that the loggers had moved on because there was nothing left worth cutting. He would live in that house over there with his mother and his uncle until it became his house, and he and his wife would farm that miserable field and repaint that house with the same white paint, and Ben would try to fix people's engines even though he wasn't very good at it, and hope he bagged a deer in the fall even though he hated hunting. Cook's Landing would be his life, whether he liked it or not. Unless he could find a way out, and there wasn't a way out that he could even imagine, let alone find.

"There she is." Ben looked up to see the bow of the *Ahmic* nosing into view as she cleared the south end of Pine Island. The *Ahmic* was one of the smaller steamers in the fleet and far from the prettiest, but it lifted Ben's heart to see her, because she'd started to become a rare sight. She was a squat, two-decked workhorse, nothing to compare with longer and sleeker beauties like the *Cherokee* and especially the *Sagamo*, jewel of the fleet, with four decks and an oak-paneled dining room with real linen tablecloths and a dozen small staterooms for the rich who wanted privacy while they steamed up the lakes. But they were all beautiful to him, even the *Ahmic.* Their steel hulls were painted gray, and their wooden upper decks and wheelhouses white, with the smokestacks a bold red and black. They carried visitors from the railhead at Muskoka Wharf up to the luxury resorts on the upper lakes, and they carried the cottagers to their cottages. They carried the mail, and hampers of fine food from Eaton's to Millionaires' Row, whose occupants were prepared to rough it, but not without pâté, and they carried supplies to the resorts and lumber and spare parts and, and — and they were serene and silent, gliding across the water, black smoke from their stacks drifting above the tree line to signal their approach. Ben worked on them now and then, when this ship or that was shorthanded and Henry could spare him. It was a filthy job, shoveling coal into the furnaces, but there was a grace to the boats that gave them a soul and made them loved, even by the crews, though you'd never get them to admit it. Watching two or three steamers rendezvous in the middle of the lake, one coming down from Lake Rosseau, the other up from town, gliding slowly toward each other then sidling up, bells clanging for "reverse" and "slow" until they were nestled side by side, transferring passengers and cargo, then easing away, a deep whistle of "so long," then bells for "full ahead"—well, it was a thing to see. And they were seeing it less and less, thanks to the Depression and the newly paved roads.

The *Ahmic* edged alongside the dock—no easy task since the *Ahmic*, small as she was for a steamboat, was still half again as long as the dock—and Ben grinned when he saw Cal Moore throwing him the bow line. Ben and Cal had been best friends till Cal's family had moved into town when his dad got a job at the paintbrush factory two years ago. Since then, the Landing had been even lonelier. Cal was as solid as Ben was slender, his open-faced grin as constant as Ben's was rare, though Ben laughed more when Cal was around. Unlike Ben, Cal got his deer every year, and he could skate rings around Ben, and did.

"You're not going to believe this, Ben," Cal yelled, as the bells sounded "All Stop."

"You're not going to believe this, Hank," Captain Corbett yelled out from the wheelhouse.

Two men rolled the gangplank onto the dock, and Ben and Henry stepped aboard and looked around. Ben scratched his head. There were boxes and crates and barrels and more boxes and more crates. There were sofas and chairs and bed frames, and they could even see paintings inside thin slatted boxes. "Paintings?" Henry shook his head. "It's a cottage, for crying out loud."

But it was a cottage that would have paintings. And crystal. And a piano.

"A piano." Henry stared at it. "Christ."

There was a lot more cursing after that. The ship was chock-full of furniture and supplies crammed into the lower deck, with a few boxes sprawled out over the upper deck as well. It had taken all morning to transfer the load from the boxcar to the steamer, and that was an easier job than getting it from the ship to the dock — taking care not to put any weight on the rotten planks — and up the steep stone steps that led from the dock to the cottage. But the new owners had booked the ship and paid the men their wages in advance, and there were six of them to handle the job, so they sweated the crates and barrels up the steps and navigated the piano — it took all of them to do it, and they wasted half an hour — and hauled up the sofas — who in this world needs two sofas? — and put together the bed frames and dropped the mattresses on the beds, though nobody was going to try to figure out where the paintings should go.

"Look at this, Ben." Cal pried open the lid of one of the crates. "I heard it sloshing."

"Lord," Ben breathed, for there were twenty-four bottles of gin in that crate — more gin than even Ernie Franks could get through. Ernie was the town drunk — well, the town drunkest — and when he was liquored up he'd weave down the middle of the main street, kicking his right leg into the air and howling with laughter, because Ernie liked to boast that he could kick higher than any man, not that there was much competition. He made it a point to know the birth date of every single soul he met, and once he learned it he never forgot. Women hated Ernie Franks, even though he was a big, lean man who'd been good looking a couple of decades ago, because if he saw one of them walking along the sidewalk he'd yell out, in his piercing baritone, "Ada Robinson, May 13, 1887! How ya doing!" He'd yell and he'd laugh and he'd call out birthdays as he kicked and careened down the street, while women ducked for cover.

Even Ernie would have been impressed by the stash of booze the new owners had brought with them. A case of gin, a case of Scotch and a case of whisky and rum, and two cases of white wine and two cases of red wine — and, oh, another case of gin.

"And olives," Ben marveled as he lugged them up the stone steps. "What do you do with twenty-four jars of olives?" Ben had never seen a jar of olives before, and now he was looking at two dozen of them.

There were other marvels in these boxes and crates. Records, a couple hundred at least, and a Victrola to play them on. The sofas were leather and so were the chairs, and Ben didn't know much about art, but the paintings were a far cry from the *Last Supper* they had hanging in the parlor at the Landing. There were landscapes with forests and lakes that sort of looked like Muskoka, and others with mountains and bears, and then others that didn't look like any-thing at all — just splotches of color that made Ben wonder if they'd been left out in the rain. The plates were china — ivory, with a band of blue and gold around the edge — and the glasses were crystal, as the sign on the outside cautioned, and the silverware was real sterling silver — and had been carefully counted, warned the note inside. "We wouldn't want her to suffer," Captain Corbett grunted, as he and Ben hauled a massive mahogany bureau up the steps.

Ben had expected the new owners to be on board, but there was only one, he was told, and she was coming up on her own. "She bought a boat from Greavette's, don't you know," Cal explained. "Said she'd drive it up herself. So we'll get to haul all this stuff back to town after she flips it over and drowns." Ben smiled. If there was anything in this world more dangerous than a cottager driving a fast boat, it was a woman cottager driving a fast boat.

However hard the work, at least the day gave Ben a chance to catch up with Cal, who was a happy guy, always laughing and joking around, the opposite of Ben, though maybe that's why they got along so well.

"So how's it going?" Cal huffed as they lugged a big leather chest up to the cottage.

"Okay. Same as always. You?"

"Okay. Hard to find a job, though. How's the Landing doing?"

"Same as always, I guess. Maybe a little worse.

So is it true you're going out with Elsie Clipsham?"

Cal flushed. "Who told you that?"

Ben grinned. The barbershop was a better source of news than the Gravenhurst *Banner*. "So it's true."

Cal tried to shrug, though it wasn't easy with both hands gripping the chest. "I dunno. Maybe."

Ben wouldn't admit how jealous he was. Elsie Clipsham was fine, if a bit big-boned. There wasn't a girl near Ben's age within five miles of the Landing, and it was starting to get to him.

"I think that's her," one of the crew called from the dock. Ben hurried down the steps to get a look. What a beauty. Long and trim, all dark mahogany, about twenty feet, the bold Greavette bow thrust out of the water, red leather seats, a tapered stern, a throaty, growling engine that said power, all you want, whenever you want it. And a scarf and sunglasses behind the wheel, an arm resting casually on the gunwale, throttle wide open.

"She's coming in too fast."

The driver throttled down, lowering the bow, and started her turn, but she should've been at dead slow by now, and she was coming in quarter speed, at least.

"What's she doing?"

"She's going to pile that thing on the rocks."

Captain Corbett pumped his arm, thumb down, warning her to slow up. But the boat kept coming in, angling now toward the dock, still way too fast. So how would this end? Ben wondered. Would she run the side of the boat up against the dock, or plow the bow onto the rocky shore? One Greavette boat lost, after a lifetime of thirty minutes on the water.

But no. At the second before the point of no return, she slipped the engine into neutral, then threw it into reverse, The motor revved, the bow heaved then settled, and there she was, flush to the dock, pretty as you please. Ben grabbed the bow line while Cal went to the stern, and Captain Corbett stepped forward to give the lady a hand, but there was no need because she was out of the boat and onto the dock in two swift steps, and she was wearing pants.

Ben had never seen his mother, or any woman for that matter, wear anything but a dress or a nightgown. But this woman was wearing beige cotton trousers and a blouse that looked more like a man's shirt. And she was tall and thin, and she had the kind of weathered tan that said she'd spent a lot of time out of doors. She reached up and slipped off her scarf, revealing a head of gray hair that now fell free, and the lines around her keen, blue-gray eyes when she took off her sunglasses and the creases in her skin, because she wore almost no makeup, suggested a woman in her fifties, with a sharp chin and high cheekbones and a tilt of the head that suggested she was used to being in charge. She must have been a looker when she was young.

The woman sized up the situation, hands on hips, half smiling. "Afternoon, gentlemen." A low, alto voice, all Scotch and cigarettes but still feminine, somehow. "Which one of you is Hank Cook?"

"That's me." Henry stepped forward and accepted her handshake.

"Ruth Chapman. Pleasure to meet you. I appreciate all the work you've been doing here."

"My nephew's been doing most of the work on your cottage." Henry nodded in Ben's direction.

"But not on the dock." She looked down at the rotten planks, frowning.

So it was egregious. "I'm sorry," Ben stammered. "There was ... we figured the house ..."

"We only had a month," Hank interrupted, in his I'm-not-going-to-take-any-lip voice, "and there was a lot to do."

"Of course there was," she answered calmly, ignoring the storm signals. "The house sat empty for four years. How bad is it?"

"Could be worse," Henry replied. "You'll be okay."

"Why don't we take a look? Thank you, gentlemen," because the *Ahmic* was getting ready to depart. Ben gave Cal a wave and a shrug and then hurried after Ruth Chapman, because she was already off the dock and climbing the steps. Ben had never seen a woman who seemed so comfortable and in charge around men.

The granite steps from the dock to the cottage passed through a thin line of birches that ringed the edge of the island, up the rocky slope, through a stand of white pine, detouring around one ancient sentinel, its trunk three feet thick — it had been there since there were only Indians on the lake, miraculously escaping the lumbermen's axe — before reaching the cottage, which was at the height of land, surrounded by pine, with a clearing in front to provide light. The place was a fair ways bigger than their house at the Landing, but still smaller than some of the mansion-cottages farther up the lake — a cedar-shingle roof, green-painted siding, a veranda along the front, large dormer windows on the second floor. Through the trees, the lake shimmered below, and a filtered sun played on the leaves and needles that carpeted the ground.

The woman took a small silver case from her cloth bag, opened it and pulled out a cigarette. A quick half-look to see if either Henry or Ben were going to offer her a light, then she fished around in her bag and extracted a pearl-clad lighter. She flipped open the lid, flicked the wheel, took a quick drag, then snapped the lighter shut. Ben knew that women smoked — he'd seen it in the movies. But he had never seen one do it outside, in front of men; the girls that did that sort of thing drank in the Ladies and Escorts section of the Albion Hotel, and it was Ben's life ambition to get in there. But Ruth Chapman didn't care where she smoked or who saw her.

"It's beautiful." She had been surveying the

cottage forever, it seemed, but it could only have been a minute; the cigarette was still fresh. Ben silently agreed. There were cottages on the lake with turrets and cupolas (as the Hitchcocks called theirs), and wrap-around verandas and fancy woodwork and huge boathouses. Pine Island didn't have a boathouse, and the cottage was hidden among the maples and pines, but there was something about it that appealed to Ben, something simple but substantial that seemed to blend with the rocks and the trees and the lake.

Ruth Chapman ground the cigarette firmly underfoot — Ben was relieved to see that she made sure there was no smoke, because the bush was tinder-dry — and walked quickly up the three steps, across the veranda and through the screen door, Ben and Henry following. She wandered slowly through the rooms, rubbing her hands along the wooden planks that lined the walls, bending down to feel the floor. The main floor consisted of four large rooms with a hallway running down the middle and stairs leading up to the second floor. On your left as you walked in was the living room — framed by windows on two sides and by a granite fireplace on the third. A doorway beside the fireplace connected to the dining room, which was wrapped in windows that looked out on the other side of the island and the main body of the lake beyond.

"Don't you love the windows in this room?" she

breathed, before passing through the French doors and across the hall into another room, lined with bookshelves and with another, smaller fireplace.

"So this is the evening room," she nodded knowingly. "Charles Wainwright designed this house, you know — that's why I bought it, sight unseen. I've always loved his homes. They're honest buildings. And he always had what he called 'the evening room' — something small, intimate, where you could retreat to at the end of the day."

It was beyond Ben's imagining that people used rooms depending on the time of day. Their house had a parlor that you never went into, unless the minister was visiting, and a kitchen where they ate and read and basically spent their indoor waking hours, and bedrooms where they slept. But here you had a room to live in and a room to eat in that wasn't the kitchen and a room just for nighttime.

Ben thought the new owner would only glance at the kitchen — the rich can't cook, which is why they hire others to do it — but she gave the stove a thorough going-over and looked around inside the walk-in pantry — the rotten planks caught her eye right away — and inspected the cupboards and the icebox, where Henry had already installed a block of ice. She looked around, spied the case of gin, pulled out a bottle and slid it into the icebox.

"First things first," she grinned, then made her way upstairs.

The master bedroom had its own fireplace, and room for chairs and a bookcase as well as a large, four-poster bed and two end tables. There were even doors leading outside to a small balcony that looked east out onto the lake.

"Wainwright always put a lot of thought into the master bedroom." She looked around with satisfaction. "He didn't believe that the lady of the house should come downstairs until after lunch." Ben said nothing but thought of his mother, who was usually up before either of the men.

She nodded in satisfaction at the big, claw-footed bathtub in the bathroom. Ben would have given anything for a house with a bathroom, for dashing to the outhouse in the dead of winter was misery, and a bath was something you took in a big metal tub that you hauled into the kitchen and filled with hot water while everyone else stayed upstairs. This bathroom had a flush toilet and a tub with actual plumbing.

"Ah, roughing it," she grinned, fishing for another cigarette, which explained that deep, raspy voice.

"But there's a lot to do here."

"Like I said—" Henry began.

"I don't like the look of the flooring on the veranda, and I counted three shutters hanging, and there's the dock, of course, and the pantry." She ignored him. "And we're going to have to repaint the outside."

"The root cellar needs work as well," Ben added.

Might as well be honest.

"So." She looked at Henry steadily. "What will it take to get you to stay here and work on the place?"

Henry shook his head. "Sorry. Have to run the Landing." And he did. It was the busiest time of the season. There were two boats tied up at the dock right now needing work.

"Well, there's your nephew ... I'm sorry, I didn't get your name."

"Ben."

"Hello, Ben." She looked at him, pulling on her cigarette, then tapping the ashes into a saucer she had brought from the kitchen. Ben flushed; he felt as if he was under inspection, which he was.

But he must have passed inspection. "Would you be interested?" she asked him after a moment. "You've done good work here already, I can tell. In four weeks, we'll have this place in shape."

"I need him at the Landing," Henry interrupted. It was true, but Ben already knew what he wanted. This woman was interesting, with her cigarettes and her slacks and her casual authority. And working on the cottage would beat running around doing stuff for Henry.

"Sorry, but—" Ben didn't know if this was a real refusal or the beginning of negotiations.

"I can pay him three dollars a day."

Ben's eyes widened, then narrowed again at Henry's warning glance. The very best guides, the ones who knew exactly where the pickerel and trout were, in sun and in rain, when the water was chilled or warm, who escorted the richest owners in their mahogany yachts, helping them with their lures and their lines — they sometimes charged two dollars a day. And she was offering a dollar a day more to a kid to help fix up a cottage.

Ben feared Henry would insist on haggling, but this was more than even he could complain about. "I guess I could manage without him."

"Good." She shook Henry's hand, then shook Ben's. Her grip was firm. "Let's start now. The lot of you have managed to put every chair and every sofa and every bed and every dresser in the wrong place. We start up here."

"I'll come back for him at six." Henry headed for the door, offering Ben only a "Don't mess this up" scowl of warning. Three dollars a day. He'd be making more than Henry made at the Landing. And this lady would be a heck of a lot more interesting to work for.

"Ben. In here." She was already dragging furniture around. He hurried in to help.

Sibelius

Each morning after breakfast he rowed over to the island in the leaky old punt that Henry had never gotten around to fixing or getting rid of. He started with the dock — if those boards weren't replaced, someone was going to go through them. Sizing, sawing and nailing down the planks took three days, and then it was on to the door of the root cellar, which took a couple of days more. His new boss seemed to pretty much ignore him; he figured she was used to having help around. But once he started work on the house, fixing the veranda and the shutters, replacing the floor of the pantry and scraping off the peeling paint, he was able to watch her, and he did watch her, closely, because she was a fascinating woman.

Fascinating to Ben, at least. She was so different from his mother, or from the teachers he'd had at school. Since his father's death, it seemed to Ben that his mother had been working more than living. Once she had loved to go out dancing, and she fussed over her hair and tilted her head back and laughed at his father's jokes. But she never laughed now, though she still smiled when Henry's latest rant amused her or she saw her son. Her hair had started to go gray over the last couple of years, and the dresses she wore had been around as long as Ben could remember, though she had had to take them in because she had gotten thinner after the accident.

"You're working yourself to death, Mary," Henry had grumbled once, which may have been a compliment, because how well and how hard you worked was how Henry defined you; Henry didn't think Ben worked hard or well enough and made sure Ben knew it. But it seemed to Ben that his mother did work harder than any of them. Henry had no skill as a farmer, and the field out back had been turning to bush before Ben's mom had taken things in hand. She plowed the field herself in the fall with the horse and plow that they borrowed from the Morrisons. Horses listened to his mother in a way they didn't listen to Ben or Henry. The next spring Ben and his mother sowed and tended and harvested the field together. She worked the vegetable garden, too, which was almost a half-acre by itself and had to be watered and weeded and protected from the rabbits and the crows. She cooked and cleaned and baked and laid down preserves and minded the store, which wasn't really a store, just a large pantry off the kitchen and a second icebox that you had to squeeze past in the front hall. It held the milk from the cows she milked herself, and the butter she churned herself, and whatever vegetables were available from the garden. There were tins of tobacco in the pantry, and canned vegetables and ketchup and toilet paper and other things cottagers might need right away and were willing to pay twice the price for rather than go all the way into town. The cottagers liked her; sometimes they'd come for a bit of rhubarb, and the next day a can of peaches, and there was no need, but they liked to sit at the table and gab while his mom gave them their change from the cash box. His mom would smile and listen and nod and sympathize, without saying very much of anything herself, which Ben noticed is what people liked in other people. But Ben remembered the laugh that he hadn't heard since the accident, and he missed it, and he missed the woman his mother had been.

The other women in Ben's life were varying degrees of stern, whether it was Mrs. Wilfrid or Mrs. White or Mrs. Cane — who loved to use one on the backsides of boys — the teachers who had come and gone at the one-room school he'd had to walk four miles to, or the widow Henkel, as everyone called her, who played the pump organ, badly, at the little Free Methodist church that they went to every Sunday — well, Ben and his mother always, because she insisted; Henry, when he was forced into it. Sometimes Ben would play his violin while the widow Henkel pumped and pounded away on the organ. She loved to shout out in rehearsal what he was doing wrong, though she hit the right notes at the right time more out of luck than anything.

There were other women in the farms and houses and shacks along the shores of the lake. They started out lively enough, most of them, but the winters and the lack of money, and the lack of hope of money, and the children that were born one after the other, even though they couldn't afford them, pressed down on them and lined their faces. None of these women was anything like Ruth Chapman. None of them even came close.

He had no idea when she smoked her first cigarette each day, because no matter how early he arrived he could smell the smoke in the cottage, even with the open windows. Much of the day she had a cigarette in her hand, though Ben noticed that she would often stub it out in an ashtray half-smoked and then a minute later light another. Lighting the cigarette, butting it out, flipping the silver cigarette case over and over with her fingers, all seemed as important as actually smoking, though he figured she still went through two packs a day. The price she paid was a rasping cough that would come on unexpectedly or after she climbed the steps up to the cottage too fast, or even sometimes if she laughed too hard.

"Damn filthy habit," she warned him, after putting away the handkerchief that she held to her mouth during coughing jags. "Wish to hell I'd never started."

She swore like that, casually. Ben had never heard his mother swear, and Henry only swore when he was mad. The crews on the steamboats swore every second word, at least when the passengers or the boss weren't around; it was like punctuation for them, or breathing. Ruth Chapman swore to give a sentence flavor, like salt. She swore the way she smoked, as a habit, but with confidence, because she was used to saying or doing anything she wanted.

She laughed, too, a dusky, deep-toned laugh that matched her alto voice. She laughed easily because she seemed to think life was something to laugh about. She laughed when she read a passage in a book that amused her — she read a lot through the day, novels mostly, by authors he'd never heard of. She'd sit on the porch in a wicker rocking chair she had brought from the city, or indoors in a big leather chair if it was rainy or the mosquitoes were bad.

"Have you read Fitzgerald?" she asked once when she caught him sneaking a look at the spine of the book she was holding. "You should read *The Great Gatsby*. Best book of the last decade, if you ask me. And Scott is a lot more fun at a party than Hemingway. Hemingway gets into fights."

He had no idea who Fitzgerald was, or Hemingway, but he figured they were famous, because she lived among the famous. Her husband had been a book publisher, and she lived in New York. "Born in Brooklyn, moved to the Upper East Side," she told him. "It's a long journey."

She read, and she worked in the cottage — she was willing and able to do her own housework, at least — and she took the boat out most days for a spin — "I love speed, don't you?" she asked him, not wanting an answer, and then laughed as she angled the Greavette up to the dock and he trotted down to grab the bow line.

And she fished, he discovered — "George and I went to Maine to fish every summer, and I always beat him, and he hated it" — so they shared one thing in common, at least, and she laughed long and hard as she pulled in a five-pound pickerel — walleye, she called them — that she had no right to be catching in the middle of the day, but pickerel were like that, sometimes.

"Would you like me to clean it for you?" he asked her as she showed it to him, proudly, one fisherman to another.

"Hell, no." She dashed its head against a rock, took a filleting knife out of her tackle box, and in five fluid motions she sliced behind the gills and along the backbone, cut the gullet and scooped out the guts, then sliced two clean fillets from gill to tail, and Ben couldn't see a single bone in either of them.

"You can clean up the guts, though," she grinned, wiping her hands on her pants before lighting a cigarette and disappearing into the cottage, where she had pickerel for lunch.

There was beer with lunch, wine with dinner, Scotch in the evening and gin in between. One way or another, there was always a drink around. He couldn't really tell if she got drunk. She never slurred her words or got all emotional, but she would laugh more, later in the day, and swear more, and talk more, because after a week or so she had started to talk to him, a rambling sort of monologue that didn't desire or require an answer: whether she should move the sofa to the other wall, what an idiot that fellow in the Ditchburn was — "he's got the whole damn lake and he still manages to almost run me over, the bloody fool" — her life in New York.

"It was Jamie Thurber who told me about this place, you know. Have you read any James Thurber? Well, he's a writer, and a damn good one. He and Andy White are the best things in the *New Yorker*, and there are a lot of good things in the *New Yorker* these days. Wish we could get it up here. So Jamie told George and me that the Carlsons had this cottage in Muskoka they were trying to unload. Distressed sale — well, we were all pretty distressed after the Crash, but the Carlsons especially. And Andy had had a cottage up here, in Dorset. Do you know where that is? Of course you do, and he'd had Jamie up a couple of years ago, and they both just raved about Muskoka. And when I heard that

Wainwright had built this place, and when I heard what the Carlsons were asking for it — well, here I am. Everyone had a huge party for me at the Algonquin, you know, the day before I left, and Dotty— Have you read Dorothy Parker? Have you read *anyone?* — well, Dotty said she'd read about my suicide in the newspapers, but I'm enjoying myself hugely. And who wouldn't? Well, Dotty, I suppose."

She loved to talk, and Ben loved to listen. New York sounded like such an exotic place — people wore different clothes to eat dinner! — and there was something about that rich, dark, raspy voice, three glasses of gin and a pack of cigarettes into the day, and a hint of an accent — but what was it? Upper East Side? Brooklyn? — that made you want to listen to her talk even if it was just about the dreadful economy and the evil of taxes, or the heat — for the June heat had been replaced by a July heat, deadening and sticky, day after day, though there always seemed to be a breeze playing around the trees near the cottage.

Every day she would play the piano for an hour or so, reading from the sheet music, and the music was fine enough, Ben thought, old and formal, though her playing seemed correct but sort of dry. She would play while Ben worked away inside or outside, not seeming to mind if he was sawing or hammering.

He came inside one afternoon, about three weeks after she'd arrived, to tell her that the floor of the veranda was fixed and ready to be painted, and found her sitting at the piano, staring at nothing.

"This is what it was supposed to be like," she said tonelessly.

"Sorry?"

"This is what it was supposed to be like. Living here, playing the piano, cheating at cards, getting old."

Ben just looked at her, confused.

"My husband and I," she explained. "This is what we had planned. And then he died on me. Damn fool."

And she went upstairs, and he didn't see her again that day.

Maybe that's why, the next day, she played the phonograph in the afternoon. Maybe there was another reason. It didn't matter.

He was scraping the paint at the front of the house. It was the last big job left, though there were lots of odds and ends to finish after that. She was changing the color of the cottage from green to dark gray — "I can't believe Wainwright would ever have sanctioned green," she maintained — and the shutters were going to be black instead of brown. Maybe it would look nicer, maybe it wouldn't; it seemed to Ben that white was probably fine for everything. But it certainly meant more work, which was good. After three weeks he had earned fifty-four dollars, taking only Sundays off to help Henry at the Landing, and that money would mean new winter clothes for all of them, and maybe another cow or a new engine for the boat; Henry hadn't decided yet. Ben knew he was doing a good job and was proud of it. Nothing egregious this time.

As he perched on a stepladder, attacking some stubborn flakes beneath the eaves of the veranda, she put on a record. It wasn't something she had done before during the day, though he'd heard music drifting across the water at night, which he had imagined signaled the switch from gin to Scotch. The Victrola didn't sound too bad (as far as he could tell from that far away) for an old-fashioned wind-up machine, which was the only thing anyone could use on the lakes, since there was no electricity.

She was having a moody day, which she had sometimes, when she talked less and drank and smoked more, and he was keeping out of her way, because she could be curt with him if he disturbed her when she was like that, and for whatever reason she wound up the machine and put the record on.

A violin. Alone. No, not alone. There were strings, pulsing beneath, quietly. The violin hovered, then ascended, like a gull surfing an updraft, trembling, suspended, then plunging down, into the guttural notes of the first fret. Instinctively, Ben's left hand flexed, searching for the fingering.

But this violin, this violinist, this music, was going

places Ben had never heard a violin go before, plunging, swooping, scampering up the scales, double-stop after double-stop — that was playing two notes at once; Ben could do it if he was careful and there was nothing hard before or after, but in a thousand years he couldn't attempt this — with a huge orchestra chasing, catching up, trying to wrestle away the music, the violin struggling to hold on.

And the music! The main tune — if that was the right word for it — was severe, like a January dawn. Other ideas came and went, interweaving, disappearing, and there! — there was the main tune again, or a snatch of it, almost hidden in the clamor. It was masterful, beyond human. The violin would take a melody, flip it on its head, while the basses grumbled below, and the orchestra would burst in, then recede, with the violin again taking the lead — long, sad, singing notes, so quiet, at times you could hardly hear — then speeding up, the notes short and sharp, as though the music was running out of time. Steely music, cold and urgent, even threatening, and now the violin was alone, dashing up and down ridiculously complicated scales, the orchestra completely silenced, in awe, then returning, asserting itself, and the struggle began again.

Impossible music, impossible notes, so far beyond anything anyone could play, yet someone was playing it. And, oh, it was beautiful, and everything else, every jig and reel and hymn and scale that Ben had played and practiced, meant nothing now compared to this, this aching, wide-open sound, this music, this real music. Ben wanted to cry, with joy, with frustration, that there could be such music, that a violin could make such sounds but he couldn't.

Swish, swish …

It was over, the violin plunging into the orchestra on one final, brassy chord. Why didn't she pick up the needle? He turned. She was standing there on the veranda, staring at him, arms folded, head slightly cocked, a smile playing around the edges of her mouth.

He blushed. "I'm sorry."

"What for? You like classical music?"

"I dunno." Pause. "I mean, yeah, I guess. Haven't heard much. Nothing like that."

"That's Sibelius."

"The violinist?"

"No, the composer. Finnish. Wrote it about thirty years ago. Not all that well-known, really, but it's my favorite. Even over the Beethoven. Especially when Heifitz plays it. That was Heifitz. He plays like the devil himself."

"Yes! Like the devil!" That was exactly it. Ambrose Heidman had told him once after one of their lessons that to really play the violin, you shouldn't play like an angel, you should play like the devil. That player had the devil in him.

"So, you like the violin?" she asked.

"Yeah. I kind of play it. But nothing like that. Just fiddle music."

She shook her head. "Playing is playing."

"Well, I just play at weddings and dances and stuff."

"So keep practicing and maybe one day you'll play the Sibelius yourself."

He shook his head. "No. There's no one to teach me."

"Ah, I guess not." And she went back inside.

She played the rest of the concerto, though this time Ben made himself keep scraping the paint, straining to catch every note. And before he left she put on some more Sibelius: the Fifth Symphony she said it was, which ended with a series of sharp blasts with huge pauses in between, so that by the end Ben was laughing.

"Of all the things that would finally make you laugh," she smiled as she lit a cigarette, watching him clean the paintbrush.

It was so strange, he thought, rowing back to the Landing at the end of the afternoon. She had never really ignored him, but she hadn't seemed all that interested in him, either. She just seemed to like rattling on about things, and he was her excuse — someone to talk to besides herself. But they had just had a real conversation, and it was about music, of all things. And she was rich and knew all these famous writers, and yet she was actually paying attention to him, because of the music.

It was different after that. He kept working, and worked hard, scraping and sanding, though he wasn't so anxious to get the job finished. Because she played music every day now, different pieces, and she'd come outside and talk to him about them.

"That's Beethoven's Emperor Concerto. For piano players like me, it's the ultimate. Nothing matches it, not even Brahms.

"This is Mozart. What do you think? Most people don't like him at first. Sometimes they never like him. Tiddly-poo music, a friend of mine calls it. But you have to have your ears on. And when you finally hear it, it's so *wise* …

"What do you think of the string quartet? A lot of people don't like chamber music. Too small-scale."

"No, no, it's great. You can hear every strand."

"Exactly."

She played the piano more now. And she started to swear if she missed a note. One morning he heard her playing as he rowed over, and a couple of hours later, while he was finishing the last of the sanding on the north side, she played the same again. She had *practiced* for him. She was performing for him. He didn't know what to make of it. Part of him was embarrassed. It wasn't right. He was just working on her cottage, that was all. But part of him liked it.

He practiced differently, now. The scales, the studies — he'd always known they mattered. But now he saw them as steps that built toward something bigger, finer. Sibelius. Except they were such small steps, steps for beginners. He tried to push himself harder, to play faster but with more precision, with less blurring of the notes. But it was hard, and there was no one to help him, and Sibelius was so far away.

He'd finished work on the cottage for the day and was already home doing the afternoon chores when Ruth Chapman visited the Landing. She had gone out in the boat and stayed gone for hours. He was on his way to the barn when he heard the growly engine of the Greavette, and the boat arced around the tip of Pine Island, full speed as always. Only, instead of heading for her own dock she was headed for the Landing, and he knew why. He hurried down to the dock as the boat eased up against it.

"John Players it is," she grinned ruefully.

That was all they had in the way of tobacco: a couple of tins of John Players Navy Cut. They kept it in the kitchen pantry, along with salt and flour and other supplies. They bought the stuff wholesale from Fielding's in town and split the profits with them. It was another way to earn a dollar, and every dollar helped.

Ruth Chapman normally smoked Dunhills, which came from England in fancy red cartons with gold lettering. She had brought half a dozen cartons with her, but already she had started to run low, and the new supply hadn't arrived yet.

"I was going to cut back," she had explained earlier that day, after asking if they sold cigarettes at the Landing. "You'd think I'd learn to stop making promises." He wished she would cut back: her coughing fits — rasping, hacking, phlegm-filled — seemed to go on forever.

"We have a couple of tins of John Players," he had told her. "But you'd have to roll your own."

"You think I can't roll my own cigarettes?" she shot back, one eyebrow raised in disapproval. "I rolled my first cigarette when I was thirteen."

So it would be roll-your-owns for awhile, but that was life at a cottage.

"Mom, this is Ruth Chapman. Mrs. Chapman, this is my mom." His mother had come out of the house as the boat neared the dock, and she was waiting by the kitchen door, wiping flour from her hands with her apron, as the two of them walked up.

Ben's mom held out her hand, still with traces of flour, offering an apologetic smile. Ruth grasped it firmly.

"A pleasure to meet you, Mrs. Mercer."

"Likewise. Won't you come in?" Ben knew how curious his mom had been about this stranger who was employing her son, knew that she had wanted to meet her for weeks but would never, ever, have tried to invent some excuse. He grinned a bit inside as the two women sized each other up: the dress, the apron, the graying blond hair neatly tied back with a cheap clasp; the canvas pants, the man's shirt with the tail in a knot, the gray hair wild from hours spent in an open boat. And the two faces: both lined, both open and intelligent, both wary, though, cautious of each other.

"Ben tells me that you have a couple of tins of tobacco for sale. I'd like to buy them."

"Of course. But won't you come in for tea? The kettle's almost boiling."

"Well, that's very kind."

Ben knew it wasn't tea that Ruth Chapman wanted at three in the afternoon. But the Landing was dry; Henry used to drink more than he should have, but he quit cold turkey four years ago, after one drunken, angry night and a shamed morning.

They stepped inside, and Ben's mom showed Ruth Chapman into the parlor, a small room with solid furniture from better times, and doilies to protect the heavy, wine-colored fabric from the grease men put in their hair when they got dressed up. The parlor was only used for company, and Ruth Chapman was the first visitor who'd been in it since the minister had come for his annual spring drop-in last May.

"Ben, would you make the tea? And bring in the tobacco." Ben hurried into the kitchen, measured out four teaspoons of tea in the strainer, dropped it into the big ceramic pot that was always on the stove and poured the boiling water from the kettle. Then he went into the pantry, pulled out the two tins of tobacco and a couple of packs of rolling papers and brought them into the parlor.

"Tea's steeping."

"Thank you, Ben. I hope this will do, Mrs. Chapman."

"Oh, it'll do fine."

"Ben, there are some sugar cookies in the tin, if you wouldn't mind bringing them in."

He did, and brought the tea in as well, using the good china cups and the silver-plated tray and milk pitcher, which he figured his mother was suggesting from the look she passed his way when she thought her guest wasn't watching. Then he retreated to the kitchen and began to reorganize the pantry, not because the pantry needed reorganizing but because he wanted to eavesdrop.

They spoke carefully, as strangers getting to know each other do, about the weather and his mom's garden.

"We've got some yellow beans ready for picking. Would you like some?"

"Of course! There's nothing like steamed beans with butter."

"No, there isn't."

"Has it been a good year for the garden?"

"Not bad. We could have used more rain."

And on like that for awhile, until …

"And how are you enjoying the cottage, Mrs. Chapman?"

"Oh, Ruth, please."

"Mary."

"I love the cottage, Mary. And thank the Lord for your son."

"I hope he hasn't been a nuisance."

"Heavens, no. He's a hard worker and good company. He has a fine ear for music."

"Yes, well, he's always loved music. He plays the violin, you know."

"Yes, I know. I must hear him play some time."

Ben's cheeks burned with embarrassment, and pleasure.

"He's fixed up the dock and the veranda, and I think in a day or two we'll have the outside painted. I'd have been sunk if it weren't for the work your son and your husband put into the place."

"Oh, Henry's not my husband. He's my brother."

"Of course. He introduced Ben as his nephew. I'd completely forgotten."

"I grew up here but moved into town when I got married. When my husband died, Ben and I moved back, and we've been here ever since."

"How long ago was that?"

"Oh, six years now. It seems so long ago. An accident in the bush."

A pause. Ruth Chapman's voice was softer, quieter.

"That's terrible. I'm so sorry."

"Well, it's been six years."

"But still."

A pause.

"Ben said you lost your husband earlier this year."

"Yes. A heart attack."

"I'm sorry, Ruth."

A longer pause. Then …

"It's funny, you know. My husband, George, he was such a serious man. I love a good party, but I had to practically drag George out to anything."

"Ben said you lived in New York."

"Yes. He owned Chapman House."

"The publishers?"

"Inherited it from his father. And he built that company up, you know, even in these times."

"That must have been very hard."

"Well, he knew business and he knew writers. And I was proud of him, and you always figure you'll have your time together, later. Then he finally decides to retire and sells the firm, and he has a heart attack. After all that, it ends with a heart attack."

"I'm so sorry."

"We'd already bought the cottage, so I decided I'd come up on my own. And it's fine. But he's not here, is he?"

"I know."

They were silent. He heard a spoon stirring in a cup.

"It's a hard thing, Mary, when your husband dies before his time."

"Oh, Ruth, that's so true."

They drank their tea, and the conversation returned to neutral subjects. Ben left the kitchen as quietly as he could, hoping they didn't know he'd been there, grabbed a pitchfork and went out to the barn.

A Party

"So that's it?"

"That's it."

Ruth Chapman walked slowly, silently, around the cottage, Ben following nervously behind. He had walked the perimeter himself that morning three times, looking for missed spots or rough patches. Scraping the paint and sanding the boards until they were smooth had been the hardest task of all. It had taken a week, with July sweat stinging his eyes. A steady ache had settled into his shoulders and never really gone away. He had come home each day with his hair covered in paint flecks, and even the long swim that he started thinking about and longing for around lunchtime didn't get it all out. But at last the sides of the house, the shutters, the veranda, the eaves — everything had been sanded baby smooth; you could run your hand along the boards and never get a splinter. And then he had laid down paint, two coats, the dark gray that she had chosen and sent away for, with black for the shutters and the trim. She was right: the gray looked better than the green, gave the cottage more style, or something like that. And he was proud of his paint job. The paint was quality, but he had applied it with care: three quick dabs, then a long stroke to smooth it out, and repeat, and repeat, the way Henry had taught him years ago. He actually wished Henry would come over to the island and look at the cottage. For once, even he might be impressed.

Still, Ruth Chapman had a critical eye, and she took her time, feeling the painted boards for bumps or air pockets, scrutinizing the slats of the shutters, peering up at the eaves. Finally, she lit a cigarette.

"Splendid."

Ben quietly let out his breath, which he hadn't noticed he'd been holding.

"You've done a grand job fixing up this place."

"Thanks. There's still a bit more to do inside."

"Yes. I'd like you to revarnish the kitchen cabinets next. But I think this house is ready for a party."

A party? This was the first she'd mentioned it. Since arriving four weeks ago, Ruth Chapman had pretty much kept to herself, playing her piano, taking the boat out, reading. She didn't seem to need company, at least any more than she got from Ben, which wasn't much, since he was working and anyway never really had much to say. Her music lessons — if that's what putting on a record and talking about the composer and the work amounted to — made up most of her daily conversation, though it was conversation Ben enjoyed.

"Yes, it's definitely time for a party," she repeated. "I've invited some friends up from New York, and the Bagnalls over at Beaumaris will be coming. Drinks and dinner Saturday night. Can you lend me a hand?"

"Sure. But —"

"But what?"

"I don't know anything about ..." He shrugged helplessly. There'd never been a party at the Landing. Around Christmas the neighbors — though the nearest of them was half a mile away — would come over for tea and Christmas treats that his mom always baked, but that was about as much excitement as they ever had, and as much excitement as Henry would tolerate.

"You can help me with the meal and serving drinks. And you should bring your violin over and play something for us."

"Oh, I don't ..." Ben shook his head.

"Well, we'll see. In the meantime, I'm going to need supplies. Can you go into town?"

"Sure."

"I'll make a list. I sent in an order awhile ago, when the *Cherokee* stopped by with the mail, so much of it you'll just be picking up."

Half an hour later he was back at the Landing, where Henry and his mother were silently eating lunch.

"I need to take the boat into town. Mrs. Chapman has given us an extra three dollars to do it." He couldn't keep the excitement out of his voice, or even explain to himself why he felt so excited.

Henry frowned. "What for?"

"To get groceries and things. She's having a party on Saturday, and she wants me to help." He couldn't help saying it like he was proud.

"What kind of help?" Henry asked, not trying to hide his suspicion.

"I'm going to help her in the kitchen and serve drinks and food and maybe play the violin."

"Well!" Ben's mom leaned back in her chair. "Imagine that."

"What do you know about helping in the kitchen?" Henry retorted. "The most you've ever done around here is peel potatoes, when we could make you."

"Oh, Henry," his mother protested. But it was true, and Ben knew it. He hadn't told Ruth Chapman, but he really didn't know anything about how to cook. He had no idea why she thought he would be of any use.

"It doesn't matter. You'll be a big help, no matter what you do." Ben was a bit surprised. His mom seemed as excited about this as he was. It was just a party, after all, just another job. But another part of him was thinking that he would be around rich people who'd be acting like rich people and partying like rich people, just like they talked about in the magazines his mom sometimes brought home when she'd been to town. It was all so … sophisticated.

"I'm going into town with you," Ben's mom got up from the table. "Come on, help me with these dishes."

"What are you going for?" Henry grabbed the remnant of his sandwich as Ben whisked his plate away from him. "And who's going to mind the place?"

"You can. You said you were going to be around all afternoon."

"That was before. I may have to go over to Acton Island now."

"No, you don't. You're going to stay here, while I go into town with Ben."

It was like that between Henry and Ben's mother. He ordered and complained and made demands, and she cooked and cleaned and listened when she had to and ignored him when she could. But when she made up her mind about something, that was final, and Henry knew it, and knew he had to go along.

"I still don't see why you have to go into town with him," he muttered, defeated.

"I'm going to make sure he gets the right groceries, and he's going to get a new shirt and pants."

"We're not going to throw away the money he's earned on foolishness!"

"He's going to be dressed right, and that's all there is to it."

"There's nothing wrong with his old church clothes."

"That's all there is to it." Henry acknowledged his defeat and registered his protest by slamming the screen door on the way out.

They didn't speak much as the old launch chugged down the lake toward the Narrows, but his mom was clearly pondering, looking out over the water and the islands, but seeing something else.

"This Mrs. Chapman really seems to like you," she said finally.

"Yeah. I guess so."

"No, you really seem to impress her. I'm proud of you." Pause. "I'll bet you'd impress a lot of people, if you were given half a chance."

"I dunno."

Compliments are always embarrassing. Compliments from a mother are the worst.

"Well, she's been all around the world, and she has money, and she knows everyone, and she likes you."

"I'm just helping out."

"I know. But people are going to notice you."

"So what?"

"I don't know so what. But things can happen."

He didn't know what to say, so he said nothing, and they were silent the rest of the way into town.

"We're going to get you a haircut," she pronounced as they walked up from the bay to the main street.

"I already had one."

"That was six weeks ago." Which should mean he was at the halfway mark. But his mother's mind was made up, and this was a day for letting her have her way.

"Thank the Lord," she muttered under her breath as they stepped into the barbershop and there was Jed. Claude, slouched in his chair, gave Ben's mom a beseeching look, then turned away in despair.

"Now, Mary, is there something special you want?" Jed asked when Ben took his place in the chair.

"Just ... well, whatever you think, Jed, but he needs to look his best."

"Then his best is how he'll look." And Jed went to work, shaping and snipping. When he was done, even Ben was impressed. The blond lick that usually fell over his face or stood nearly on end when he swept it away impatiently now rested in a comfortable wave across the top of his forehead. If only it would stay that way.

"Thank you so much, Jed." His mom gave him an extra fifty cents, which was quite a tip.

"You take care now, Mary." He offered his sad, gentle smile.

From there it was straight to McJannet's for a new white shirt and a pair of gray wool pants. He'd be hot in the pants in the summer, but they were practical because he could use them for church or when he was playing in public.

Then came the grocery shopping. "Do you know what she's making?" Ben's mom frowned as she scanned the list.

"It's called *boeuf bourguignon*." He tried to remember how she'd pronounced it.

"What's that?"

"I think it's stew."

Mostly they just went from store to store, picking up orders that had already been prepared. Ruth Chapman must have been planning the party for awhile, because some of the ingredients had come all the way from Toronto by special order.

"Garlic." Maude Fielding shook her head as she handed it over. "Can't stand the stuff."

Not only garlic, but capers and tiny pearl onions, something Ben had never seen before, and mushrooms and real tomatoes that must have been grown in greenhouses because it was weeks before the ones in their own garden would be ready and four pounds of stewing beef that Passmore's had specially chopped and trimmed for the occasion. And roses — long-stemmed red ones — that had come up that very morning on the train. "Can you imagine such a thing?" Mrs. Montgomery asked in wonder at the station, when they picked up the order.

It took both of them to get everything down to the boat, and Ben's arms ached from the eight full bags of groceries and supplies he had carried all that way. His mom looked as if she needed a rest, too, and they hardly talked at all on the trip back. Ben dropped his mom off at the Landing and then carried on to Pine Island, where Ruth Chapman was waiting for him.

"There you are. Now, let's take a look at that beef."

By the time he reached the kitchen, weighed down with bags of groceries, she was already throwing bones from the butcher into a large pot of boiling water.

"That's a fine butcher you have in town," she declared while he put things away. "Now listen. Do you know how to open a bottle of wine?"

Ben shook his head.

"And I'll bet you can't mix a Scotch and soda very well, either. Never mind. You'll learn in no time." And she grabbed a bottle of red wine from a case beside the icebox.

"This is a corkscrew. You use this part to cut the foil, like so … now you centre the corkscrew and turn, and turn … now you take this part and prop it against the edge, like so, and you lever it until … Voila!" And she poured herself a glass of wine.

It went on like that for more than an hour: "Remember, you always pour the wine from the guest's right side, and you only fill it two-thirds full … use a shot glass, but don't worry if you go over the line, just never go under it … what do you mean you've never seen a lime before? The British Empire was built on limes. Prevents scurvy. Well, here's how you cut them … So, three parts tonic water to one part gin, same with Scotch and soda or rye and water …" And Ruth Chapman instructed Ben in the arts of bartending while she chopped and threw vegetables and herbs into the pot of simmering beef stock and prepared a marinade for the beef and smoked and drank and listened to Schubert. Schubert seemed to Ben like Mozart, only with backbone.

He returned the next morning right at eight to find that she already had a list of things that needed doing, including washing all the sheets on the beds in a tub with P and G soap and a washboard — the hardest job known to man or, usually, woman — and hanging them to dry on a clothesline, after he'd rigged the clothesline. Then she brought him into the kitchen and put him to work helping her wash the china and crystal and polish the silver that made no sense at a cottage.

"I'll go anywhere on earth but not without my crystal," she replied to the question he hadn't asked, as she carefully ironed a damp linen tablecloth.

In the middle of the afternoon she sent him back to the Landing to get cleaned up. His mother had hot water waiting for a bath.

"I'm just going to jump in the lake."

"No, you're not. You're taking a proper bath."

"You're going to make him take a bath?" Henry was astonished. "It's eighty-five degrees outside."

"Henry!"

"I never heard of such a thing," Henry snorted in

disgust, and for once Ben agreed with him. But it was better to bathe than argue, and though he only shaved once a month, and then mostly for encouragement, he shaved anyway and put on the new clothes that his mother had laid out for him, carefully pressed. She combed his hair, while he squirmed in protest, until she had it in a fair imitation of Jed's masterpiece, and then — finally! — stepped back and inspected him.

"Don't you look handsome," she smiled.

"Mom …" he protested, and headed for the door.

"Don't forget your violin."

"I guess."

He had been debating whether to take it. After all their talk about music, he was nervous at the thought of playing in front of Ruth Chapman, not to mention her guests, and he'd pretty much decided to forget to bring the thing. But his mother insisted.

"Take it with you. And play something nice."

"I dunno. Maybe."

She stood in front of him and put her hands on his shoulders.

"Now you listen to me. I want you on your best behavior tonight."

"Okay." Frankly, the whole thing was starting to terrify him.

"Ben." She looked at him. "Tonight is important. Maybe … who knows? Just do what Mrs. Chapman asks, and don't speak out of turn, and play your violin if they ask, and … and make a good impression, that's all."

"Sure."

She sighed as he bolted out the door.

"Well." Ruth Chapman looked Ben over as he stood before her awkwardly in the kitchen. "You dress up right fine. Please pass on my compliments to your mother."

"Sure."

She smiled. "And I'm glad to see you brought your violin. So, let's lay out the table."

And he learned how to fold napkins, and where the dessert fork went, and why some wineglasses had long stems and some had short.

"They're here."

The *Cherokee*, with two deep blasts on her whistle, approached the island. Ben and Ruth went down to meet it, and Ben held the rope while the boat gingerly edged up to the end of the dock, where two hands lowered a small gangplank.

A thin man of about Ben's height, in his forties, with thick glasses and a sharp, creased face. Beside him a woman, thin and bony, but pretty, too, with soft brown hair and a warm smile. Behind them, two men, both in their twenties, both with blond hair, both in pale linen shirts and cotton pants, both squinting against the sun.

"Perry!" Ruth Chapman threw open her arms and embraced the thin man, who scowled.

"Lovely to see you, too, Ruth, but, my God, they had no booze on that boat."

"Or on the train," the man's companion smiled. "He's been impossible since lunch."

"Helen." Ruth and the woman gave each other quick, affectionate hugs. "It's so good to see you again. And Chester! How lovely."

"Hello, Aunt Ruth. Thanks for asking us. This is my friend Tad."

"Lovely to meet you, Tad."

Ben was trying to grab hold of as many of the dozen suitcases as he could. Each one weighed a ton.

"Would you boys give Ben a hand? Ben, this is my nephew Chester, and his friend Tad. And this is Perry Larchworth and Helen Turnbull. Perry is the best reporter at the *New York Times*."

"Oh, Ruth …"

But Ben was confused. Larchworth was lightly touching the woman's arm, but she wasn't his wife, yet they'd traveled together …

Oh. Sophisticated.

"Hello."

"Hello."

"Here, we can carry those."

"Where's my drink?"

Ruth Chapman led them — Ben and Chester and his friend straining under the weight of the suitcases — up the stone steps to the cottage and gave her guests the full tour, while Ben took the drink orders, with Larchworth first.

"Martini. Make it a double. Hold the vermouth. Hold the olive."

"So, just a glass of gin?"

"You got it, son."

He mixed the drinks and brought them to the guests as they took chairs on the veranda. He was nervous, even though she'd made him practice (she drank the experiments) and had left written instructions on the counter. Ben had never been around alcohol — when Henry used to drink, he did it in his room because he was ashamed — and didn't know its rituals and assumptions. But no one winced as they sipped their gins and Scotches and talked and chatted and laughed — mostly at what Larchworth was saying.

"So I'm standing there in the doorway, and this girl is falling off the mayor's lap, and he's beet red, and he shouts at me, 'You don't understand — she's underprivileged!' Hey, I could use another drink."

Did everyone in New York drink this much? Ben wondered. But it wasn't his job to wonder, or even listen. Ben got Larchworth another drink and then went back to the kitchen, where he cleaned and peeled potatoes and carrots for seven, and prepared the lettuce for the salad, and sliced the cheeses and pâtés that had come all the way from Toronto via Fielding's grocery, and placed them on trays, and went out to refill glasses, while Ruth Chapman came inside and rearranged all the trays, reminding him of the need for biscuits with pâté and cheese. She grinned when he blushed, and then took the trays outside. He only slipped up once, mixing a drink wrong, so that Larchworth's friend Helen winced when she tasted it. "Let me take that." Ruth Chapman whisked away the glass and led Ben back to the kitchen. She gave the drink a sniff. "Gin and tonic is God's gift to summer. Gin and soda is an abomination." But she didn't sound angry as she watched him prepare a fresh drink. "You're doing fine," she smiled before returning to her guests, taking the new drink with her.

Ben heard a boat pulling up to the dock and ran down to help the Bagnalls. Bruce Bagnall was a big man with huge shoulders who might have played football a couple of decades ago, though most of the pounds now weren't muscle. Violet Bagnall was way too thin and way too blond, and her dress was way too red and clingy for a cottage.

"Everybody, this is Bruce and Violet Bagnall." Ruth made the introductions. Larchworth looked at the husband skeptically.

"Ruth says you're the richest man on this lake."

"Well, I don't know about that …"

"She says I'm the best reporter at the *New York Times*, and I am, so you must be the richest man on the lake."

"I've done all right."

"I'll bet there's a story behind that."

"Not really."

"And I'll bet you never talk to reporters."

"Never."

"So it's going to be a long night."

"Perry, have another drink."

And Ben retreated again to the kitchen.

The kitchen was drenched in the smell of beef and wine from the stew, whatever it was called, simmering away in the oven. When the time came, Ben put the potatoes on to boil, and later the carrots, and he sliced the bread and buttered it, and then everyone moved from the veranda to the dining room. Ruth Chapman arrived in the kitchen to make a salad dressing from vinegar and olive oil and toss the salad.

As the guests came into the house for dinner, Ben could hear the conversation had taken a turn.

"I tell you, it's the taxes." That was Bruce Bagnall, his voice raised. "The hard times would be over in six months if the federal government would stop taxing us to death."

"Tell me more about your suffering, Bruce."

"Now look here —"

Ruth Chapman sighed. "Perry has decided he doesn't like Bruce, and he's already had four martinis, so this dinner is probably going to be a disaster." Then she winked at Ben. "But disasters can be so much fun."

Who can figure out such people? Ben thought to himself as he removed the beef from the oven. He helped her spoon the food onto the plates and take the plates out to the guests, and poured the wine so they could toast.

"To the king."

"To Franklin Roosevelt."

"I'm not toasting a Communist!"

"And I'm not toasting a Brit!"

"Thank you, Ben," Ruth Chapman said, and he took his cue and went back into the kitchen, where he fixed a plate of food for himself, as she'd told him he could. The stew astonished him: rich and smooth and subtle. Nothing his mother had cooked had ever come close.

Dinner was long and loud, and when they weren't yelling at each other they were laughing, and they yelled louder and laughed louder as Ben opened and poured the fourth bottle of Bordeaux. Ben wasn't sure they even noticed the blueberry pie and ice cream that Mrs. Orton had made special at Smalley's. Ben had most of the dishes washed and put away by the time Ruth Chapman proposed, "Why don't we have our brandy in the living room?"

He brought out the brandy glasses and carefully poured from the heavy crystal decanter where she kept — she had assured him — only the very finest cognac. When he came into the living room with the tray of glasses, he saw that Larchworth had launched into another story, and everyone was listening and laughing. Even Bruce Bagnall was red-faced.

"So the cop says he died at the scene, but the doc says they revived him in the ambulance, and my editor's standing there in the newsroom screaming at the top of his lungs. 'I don't care what it takes! I want him dead by the next edition!'"

"Damn, but you're funny, Larchworth."

Ben found himself laughing, too, as he listened while this wildly animated man with the thick glasses paced around the room and waved his arms and even jumped up on furniture, telling stories of gin joints and crooked cops and even crookeder politicians. Eventually he collapsed into a chair, exhausted, and everyone else was exhausted, too, from laughing so hard.

"Did you know that Ben here plays the violin?" Ruth Chapman told her guests. "I'm told he's very good."

"Oh, really? Helen asked, with an encouraging smile.

"Oh, really?" Bruce Bagnall asked, without the slightest interest.

Ben flushed. He had forgotten about the violin,

what with dinner and all. Besides, he didn't really want to play, especially after Perry Larchworth had enthralled everyone for almost an hour.

"I don't really play much," he mumbled.

"Yes, you do," Ruth Chapman contradicted him. "You practice every morning in the toolshed. Your mother told me."

"The toolshed?" Larchworth raised an eyebrow. "Is it the acoustics?"

"Why don't the two of you play something together?" the nephew, Chester, suggested. "You know we love to hear you play, Aunt Ruth."

"No you don't, but it's sweet of you to pretend, Chester." Ruth Chapman got up. "Come on, Ben, why don't we play a duet?"

"Oh, I —"

"Come on, son," Larchworth called out. "We were put on this earth to suffer."

"Consider it an order." And Ruth Chapman headed for the piano.

Ben slouched out to the kitchen, retrieved the violin and slouched back. He tried to tune it as quickly as he could, because everyone was watching, while Ruth practiced a couple of scales.

"Ben, do you know 'Flow Gently, Sweet Afton?'"

"Sure." It was one of his mother's favorite tunes. Ruth Chapman improvised an introduction in the key of D. She looked up. Ben raised his bow and began to play.

He was awkward at first, his fingers felt stiff, and his nervousness trembled down his arm. But it was a lovely tune, as soft and flowing and gentle as the Scottish stream it described. And it was a pleasure to have such a fine accompanist. He noticed that Larchworth had cocked his head to one side, listening intently. Ben heard the lyrics of the song in his head, tried to make the violin sing the sense of those lyrics.

Flow gently, sweet Afton, among thy green braes,
Flow gently, I'll sing thee, a song in thy praise,
My Mary's asleep by thy murmuring stream,
Flow gently, sweet Afton, disturb not her dream …

They played it through, and when they finished the applause was real, and Ben couldn't help smiling a bit, because they had been really good.

"You have a beautiful sound," Helen Turnbull told him.

"It's the toolshed," Larchworth interjected. "All the greats started out in toolsheds." Ben blushed, but it didn't seem as if Larchworth was making fun of him the way he'd been making fun of Bagnall, who seemed to have forgotten how angry he'd been an hour before.

"Play some more!" Bagnall shouted. He'd liked the music after all. "Encore!"

But most of what Ruth Chapman knew he didn't

know, and most of what he knew — reels and jigs and other square-dance music — was foreign to her. They played a couple of rousing hymn tunes, and the cottagers across the lake must have wondered why people were singing — more like yelling — "Guide Me, O Thou Great Jehovah" at a cottage, but there was an appetite for something more fun.

"Play some of your square-dance music, Ben. Give us a tune." Ruth got up from the piano.

"All right." He didn't mind now. In fact, he kind of liked having everyone listen to him play. "This is 'Ragtime Annie.'"

He tapped his right foot four times to give himself the beat, and away he went.

Larchworth let out a whoop, and the guests started clapping along. This was his kind of music, the kind he loved to play, and he was good at it, and he knew it, and they knew it, too. It was toe-tapping music, music you couldn't listen to sitting down, music that made you just want to grab someone and swing them around.

"Woo-hoo!" Chester's friend Tad yelled, when Ben had foot-stomped to a finish.

"You boys move that couch," Ruth Chapman commanded. "We're going to have a dance."

Now they were in his element, listening to his music and dancing to it, like everyone did on a Muskoka Saturday night, if they could. With barely a pause for breath, Ben launched into "The Girl I Left behind Me."

"The kid needs a drink." Larchworth emerged from the kitchen, carrying a bottle of beer along with a very large martini — well, glass of gin — he'd poured himself.

"Oh, no, I —"

"One won't hurt," Ruth Chapman smiled. "We don't want you to overheat."

So he took a sip — it was bitter, like liquid oatmeal without brown sugar, but it cooled his throat — and then gave them the "Peekaboo Waltz," a lovely tune in three-quarter time. The men took turns waltzing the three women around the room, then stomped their feet and began twirling each other when he switched to "The Crooked Stovepipe," an old square-dance favorite. They couldn't square dance to save their lives. But they were having an enormous amount of fun, though it was a typically hot, muggy night, and before long everyone was sweating and Ben's beer was gone, but that was okay because someone brought him another.

They didn't want to stop, and he didn't want to stop, either. He went through them all: "St. Anne's Reel" and "Maple Sugar" and "When the Moon Comes over the Mountain" and "When It's Springtime in the Rockies." Sometimes, Ruth

Chapman would recognize the tune and sit back down to the piano and chord along. Other times, she danced up a storm, though it was a strange thing to see a grown woman jig with a cigarette in her hand. Larchworth managed to drink while he was dancing, which might have had something to do with his lurching from side to side from time to time.

Sometimes Ben would play a popular tune, like "By the Light of the Silvery Moon" or "Carolina Moon" that everyone would recognize, and they'd stop dancing and sing along. (No matter what he sang, the nephew was notoriously off-key.) It went on like that for a couple of hours, until they were all too hot and sweaty and exhausted to keep going, and the Bagnalls declared that they had to get back to their cottage, and the others decided it was time for bed.

Ben felt elated, and giddy, and light-headed, and strange, and suddenly in need of air. He stepped out onto the veranda to catch his breath. Make an impression, his mother had told him. Well, he'd made an impression. He'd made them sing and dance, and singing and dancing was the very best thing you could do if you were having a party, better even than beef stew with a fancy name.

Ruth Chapman had escorted the Bagnalls of Beaumaris down to the dock and their boat. He didn't know if she wanted him to stay and help clean up. She wasn't coming up from the dock, so he headed down. It was strange, though, the path seemed steeper and harder to navigate, even though he'd done it a thousand times.

He found her standing at the end of the dock, gazing up at the Milky Way, its broad, pale band arcing across the night sky from tree line to tree line.

"Should I … do you want me to wash or dry or … something?" he asked.

Ruth Chapman looked away from the stars and peered at him.

"How many of those beers did you have?"

"I dunno. A couple. A few."

"Too many." She shook her head. "Your mother is not going to be happy with me in the morning."

"Yes, she will. She wanted me to make an impression."

"And you did." She smiled. "You were the life of the party."

"I love to play."

"It shows."

"Ruth!" Larchworth yelled down from the cottage. "How about one last nightcap?'

"Up in a minute, Perry." Then she turned back to Ben.

"It's a shame, really."

"What?"

"That there's no one here to teach you properly."

"I know! There's so much I don't know how to play, but I could play it, I know I could, if someone would just show me."

"Well, maybe you'll get to Toronto some day. I'm sure they have some fine teachers there."

"No, I'll never get to Toronto. I'll never get away from this lake."

She didn't catch the resignation in his voice. "Well, who would want to? It's so beautiful."

"Not now it's not."

That surprised her. "What do you mean?"

"Now it's summer, and it's tame." He looked out over the dark water. "It's a big pond, and people play on it — go swimming and boating, and they sit beside it and it looks really pretty. But you should see it when it's beautiful."

"When is that?"

"November. Everyone's gone away, and the lake is ours again, and all the leaves are gone, and everything is brown and gray and hard, and the lake is gray and choppy, and snow falls on it, and you can barely see the islands through the snow. That's when the lake is beautiful."

He didn't know about the effects of beer. He just knew that suddenly he wanted to talk, could talk all night.

"Sometimes in January, when there's a white sun — through the clouds, you know? — and the lake is froze over and you can't hear a single sound except your feet crunching the snow — sometimes, like that, it hurts, it's so silent and frozen, and you're so alone."

He hadn't rambled on like that since his father died.

Ruth Chapman was smiling again.

"You are an artist, Ben Mercer."

"Huh?"

She stepped close to him and leaned forward and kissed his cheek. He didn't move.

"Now get yourself home to bed."

He climbed into the punt and, fumbling, untied the ropes. She gave the boat a playful push with her foot.

"Good night, Ben."

"Good night."

And he rowed, unsteadily, across the brief stretch of water that separated the two of them, and wondered whether he really was an artist, and whether he ever would really learn to play the violin, and why she had kissed him.

Limits

Pain.

Pain even before light, even before he opened his eyes, which brought more pain. Pain that seized his temples and squeezed, making the blood pound, which made the pain worse. He groaned, closed his eyes, rolled onto his side, curled into a ball. What would it take to make the pain go away?

"Aren't you up yet?" Henry called from the bottom of the stairs. "What's the matter with you?"

"I'm sick," Ben moaned from beneath the sheets. But he wasn't sick. He was dying.

He heard Henry clumping up the stairs, heard him come into his bedroom, and suddenly the sheets were gone and Henry was standing over him.

For a moment, he didn't say anything. Then, "Go throw yourself in the lake. Right now."

The pain of cold on top of the pain of pain? It seemed more than Ben could live through. But the prospect of living didn't hold much appeal right now, so he rolled out of bed, waited for the whirling room to steady, decided he probably wouldn't throw up, then groped his way into his swim trunks. He knew Henry and his mom were watching him as he made his way through the kitchen, but he kept his head down, shamed, sullen. Outside, he winced at the piercing sun as he made his way gingerly down to the dock. Then — good-bye — he plunged into the lake. The early August water was practically tepid, but it was enough in his fragile state to shock his system, forcing the air out of his lungs, forcing him to surface. Still, the pain wasn't quite so bad.

He swam a few desultory strokes but soon gave up, contenting himself with just treading water, every now and then disappearing again beneath the surface, where the world was blissfully cooler and darker, until he was forced up for air.

"Ben," his mother called. "Come and get your breakfast."

Breakfast. Oh, God.

She was waiting for him with a towel and a shirt when he reached the kitchen, and he was grateful for both. But just the smell of the plate of fried eggs and bacon waiting for him made his stomach heave. The thought of actually eating it was intolerable.

"You're going to eat your breakfast. All of it. And that's all there is to it."

He slumped into his chair, picked up a fork with a trembling hand and scooped up a mouthful of egg. There was a moment of great danger, but the moment passed.

"How did you manage to get drunk last night?" Henry demanded. "You were supposed to just be helping with the food."

"Somebody gave me a beer because it was hot," Ben replied, squinting warily at the bacon before him.

"It was a whole lot more than one beer," Henry shot back. To be honest, Ben couldn't remember how much he'd had to drink. He only knew that he was never going to drink again as long as he lived, if he lived.

His mom seemed more upset than angry. "I told you to make a good impression, and look what you did."

"I did make a good impression," Ben protested. "I played the violin for hours, and they danced, and somebody kept giving me a beer, and that's how ..." He gratefully gulped the coffee that his mother had poured for him.

"Well, I don't know who these people are, giving liquor to a fifteen-year-old boy." Henry attacked his bacon savagely with his fork. "I have a mind to go over there —"

"Oh, really," his mother said, exasperated. "As if you think I don't remember when you came home soused from that dance at Walker's Point."

"That was different," Henry grumbled. "I was sixteen."

"It was your birthday."

"That's not the point."

"The point is it's over." His mother started to collect

the dishes. "Are you supposed to go over there today?" she asked Ben.

He shook his head, carefully. "Nah, not till Tuesday, after everyone's left."

"Good." Henry got up from the table. "You can catch up on some of the work you're behind on here. Starting with the barn. I want you to muck it out and lay down fresh hay."

The barn, it turned out, was as good a place as any for throwing up.

Ben wished he was over there, though. He saw them, as the sun lowered in the sky, sitting out on the dock, drinks in their hands, laughter rippling across the water as Larchworth paced the dock, arms windmilling. He had played music for them, and they had danced for him, and he had talked to them, and they had called him by his name and given him a beer, or two, or whatever — they had served *him* when he was supposed to be serving them. He had become part of their group last night, almost one of them; he had almost belonged.

And he had talked to Ruth Chapman, really talked to her, confided in her. They had only talked about the lake, but he felt as though he had told her about his whole life, that she understood, that this place was beautiful, yes, but it was also a trap. She had called him an artist, had talked about Toronto, as though she knew, she *knew* that he had to get out, as though she *wanted* him to get out.

And she had kissed him. Just on the cheek, almost the way his mother had kissed him when he was younger, but not quite. He didn't know what it meant. Did she mean it as a real kiss? He shuddered. Whatever else Ruth Chapman was, she was older than his mother. But it wasn't that kind of a kiss anyway. More, playful. More ... to make him feel she understood, she cared. He wanted to be back over there, wanted to be with them on the dock. He didn't belong at the Landing. He belonged over there.

Monday afternoon, the *Segwun* — as big as the *Cherokee* but not as elegant — pulled up to the Pine Island dock, and Ruth Chapman's guests returned to Toronto. When he arrived at the cottage the next day, she was still in bed, but there was a note reminding him to sand and varnish the kitchen cabinets, so he set to work. It was after one before she appeared.

"Good afternoon."

"Afternoon."

"I hope you enjoyed yourself Saturday night."

"Oh, yeah. I had too much beer, though."

"Yes. Sorry about that." And she went out to the veranda with a book.

It was like that for the next week, and it confused him. She wasn't unpleasant or anything. She just seemed to ignore him, as though he wasn't there. She stayed in her room more often, or went out for long rides in the boat, or read. But there was no music and little conversation. And when he had finished with the cabinets, later that week, she told him that, really, there wasn't much to do around the place, but she would send word if she needed him.

"Okay. Well, I'll see you, then." He shuffled his feet.

"I'm sure you will." She offered a formal smile, and that was that.

Was it the kiss? He'd been drunk, and she might have been drunker than normal, and though it had seemed strange, it hadn't bothered him. But maybe it had bothered her. He wanted to say something, tried to think of a way to bring it up, to say it was okay. But how could he? She didn't seem to want to talk about it.

And now she didn't even seem to want him around. It tore at him. He had gotten used to her, hearing her talk about music and books and New York and everything that nobody talked about at the Landing. He had gotten used to looking in on her life, almost as though it was his life, too, or could be, one day. His mother was right: things happen, or they don't. And if they don't, then you're stuck, you don't go anywhere. He thought he had made a good impression, thought he had made her interested in him, in his future. What had gone wrong?

Worst of all, he was back to life with Henry, to the short, sharp orders, the drudgery of work. No music. Just silent resentments.

"When you're done that, your mother wants you to weed the garden … When you're done that, you can feed the hens … When you're done that, you can give me a hand with the Hitchcocks' boat."

Working on that boat — cleaning and polishing the leather, carefully waxing and polishing the fine mahogany, helping tune the massive engine — brought him to close quarters with Henry for the first time in weeks. They worked badly together, as they always did, bumping into each other, getting in each other's way. Henry lost his temper a lot, and Ben said "Sorry" a lot and wondered sometimes whether Henry was deliberately trying to provoke him.

But Ben's mind was on other things, things he had only half wished before but that now seemed almost reachable. Working away, raking this and scraping that, the dreams would come. There were violin teachers in Toronto, Ruth Chapman had told him, good ones, who could teach him to play properly. The lessons would be expensive, but maybe if he got a job and lived really cheaply he'd be able to afford them. Maybe he'd even be able to afford a new violin, one that wasn't falling apart, that didn't play the notes raw. He'd be sixteen in February, old enough to live on his own. Maybe he should just get out of here while there was still time.

And then the doubts would come. There were a lot of men out of work. What kind of job could he do that others couldn't do better? And who says that any teacher would offer to give lessons to a kid who played the fiddle and couldn't play much more than jigs and reels? And what if Ben couldn't afford what it cost?

And then the guilt would come. Henry couldn't afford to hire help, and he couldn't handle everything on his own. Henry needed Ben, and Ben knew it, and they both resented it. And more than Henry, there was his mother. He'd be leaving her alone — worse, he'd be leaving her alone with Henry. To move out, to leave her at the Landing, what would there be for her?

It's *my* life, he'd say to himself, furiously pitching hay at the startled cows, I can live it any way I want. Except he knew it wasn't his life. His life belonged to others, everyone's life did. He was needed here, wanted, even, though he'd never get Henry to admit it. That was the claim the Landing had on him. That, as his mother would have said, was all there was to it.

He wanted to talk to Ruth Chapman, let her see his dilemma. Maybe she had a way out. Maybe she could help him. But she didn't seem interested in him anymore. And that was the worst thing of all. There were chores he could do over there, work she could find for him if she really wanted to. Why wouldn't she? Why was she ignoring him?

It was almost two weeks before he saw Ruth Chapman again, and when he realized her boat was headed for the Landing rather than her cottage, he practically ran down to the dock so he could be waiting for her by the time she pulled up.

"Hi." He even made a point of smiling.

"Hello," she smiled back. "How are you keeping?"

"Okay."

"Good. Is your uncle around, by chance?"

His uncle? What did she want with Henry?

"Yeah, he's up at the house."

In fact, Henry was coming down from the house to the dock.

"Afternoon."

"Good afternoon. And how have you been keeping?"

"Well enough, I suppose."

"That's good to hear. I was wondering how busy you and Ben are right now."

"Busy enough."

"Well, I'm having another party." Ben's heart leapt. She would want him to help out. Maybe he'd get to play the fiddle again.

"It's a large party," she went on. "Thirty guests, at least. And I'm worried about the steps leading up to the cottage from the dock. We need to make them a bit more ... predictable, if you know what I mean."

"I guess so."

The steps were really just slabs of rock embedded at more or less regular intervals in the slope leading up to the cottage. It was easy enough to trip on them, especially going down, if you weren't watching or you'd had too much gin.

"How long do you think it would take the two of you to build a proper stone staircase?'

"That depends. We'd have to order the stones and get our hands on a cement mixer —"

"Already done and waiting for you in Bracebridge."

"Then maybe a couple of weeks. It's a big job."

"Then you'd better get started right away. The party is Labor Day Saturday," which was just over two weeks away. "Can I count on the two of you, six dollars a day?"

Ben gave Henry a quick look. The summer was winding down, and jobs were getting fewer. And six dollars a day! They'd have done it for half that.

Henry obviously agreed, though he'd be damned if he'd show it. "I guess we could manage it."

"That's splendid. So you can start tomorrow?"

"I suppose so."

"That's it, then. Good to see you again, Ben."

And she slipped the idling motor into reverse, and backed away.

The next day they set to work early, digging out the old steps, pulling up grass and rocks and smoothing the slope and then pounding the ground flat with shovels. Then it was into Bracebridge with the scow hitched to the launch to pick up the granite slabs and cement and a cement mixer and crushed stones for drainage from O'Neill's. It took Ben three trips and a long day to ferry everything to the island, where Henry was already at work spreading the crushed stone. Then came day after day of work: smoothing the stones with a hammer and chisel, mixing the cement, fitting the risers and skirtboards that held the steps in place, fitting the stones and troweling in the cement around them, then starting all over again. It was a hard, sweaty job, and the late-August mosquitoes were as plentiful as the late-August heat was unusual. By now, the first cool waves of approaching autumn should have started to sharpen the night air. But not this year. This summer didn't seem to want to end.

He was working with Henry, and that was never comfortable. At first it was the same old "Watch yourself" and "Sorry." But after a couple of days Ben started to get the hang of it, and there was something about working with the stone — shaping and fitting the pieces together and anchoring them with cement — that he started to enjoy. Watching the staircase progress, step by step, was somehow deeply satisfying, something you could see, appreciate, something that would last.

And Henry was a natural as a stonemason. He could chip away at a stone and fit it beside another as though they were pieces of a jigsaw puzzle that he held in his head. Ben couldn't help admiring the skill in Henry's hands, his sharp eye, his steady judgment about which piece should go where.

It was strange that Henry didn't seem to enjoy the work any more than he enjoyed any other work. For him, building a set of steps was the same as fixing an engine or slaughtering a pig. It was all work.

That's when Ben began to realize. Henry wasn't angry at Ben; he was angry at the Landing, or the cottagers, or the bank. He was angry at everything, because everything was against him. Maybe, if Ben had shared that anger, the two of them would have gotten along better. But Ben wasn't angry at the whole world. Not yet. Ben suspected that Henry didn't like living at the Landing any more than he did, resented the isolation, resented being poor. And Henry didn't love the lake, didn't swim in it — couldn't, because of his bad leg — and he didn't have a fiddle or something else that would allow him to get his mind off things. Henry's mind was always on things. Just like Ben's was now.

Ruth Chapman was keeping to herself. Once a day, or maybe twice, she'd come down, look at what they were doing, congratulate them on their progress, and then retreat to the cottage. She didn't seem to want to talk to Ben. Well, how could she, with Henry around? But he had the feeling she wouldn't have wanted to talk anyway. She just wasn't talking to him anymore. It made his stomach ache, along with his back.

While they worked, things arrived, and people, mostly on the *Cherokee*, which was doing the daily Lake Muskoka run. Workers navigated boxes and crates around the still-unfinished steps, casting resentful glances at Henry and Ben for making their task so much harder. One day they wrestled a table up the slope — a long flat slab of dark wood and three trestles to rest it on, and dozens of collapsible wooden chairs. If the weather was nice — and it would be a disaster if it wasn't — the guests would eat on the patch of cleared land in front of the veranda. A formal dinner beneath the Muskoka pines, lit by lanterns — candles in tinted glass hanging from hooks. Ruth Chapman asked Ben and Henry to drill the hooks into the trees so the lanterns would light the stairs and the clearing. It was going to look really pretty.

Another day there were cases of wine, red and white, and more Scotch and more gin, and many cases of food — cheese and flour and sugar and chocolate and other ingredients for fancy things with French names. A third day featured silver trays, porcelain bowls and tureens, more china and silver and crystal and linen. On the Thursday before the party, with the steps mostly built and the concrete mostly set, it was more food: three large roasts of prime beef packed in ice, a bushel basket of new potatoes, another of fresh-picked peas, and apples and oranges and grapes, imported from who-knows-where, and lettuce and olive oil in glass jars and vinegar and seasonings and … Ben lost track of it all as he helped cart it from the steamer to the house. Friday it was people from town who came to clean and wash and scrub. Ben was a bit offended that she didn't trust him to do it, but Ruth Chapman wanted the house spic and span from attic to root cellar. She let him pitch in, though, because the staircase was finally done, a lovely set of granite steps, brownish pink, ascending from the dock to a small landing, then turning left and rising to the clearing in front of the cottage. He was proud that he had helped build them, because they would last for decades. It was one of the few things he and Henry had done together that Ben had almost enjoyed, however much his back resented it.

He was standing there, admiring their handiwork, when the flowers arrived, dozens of bouquets — roses and gladiolas and carnations in elaborate arrangements — that had been shipped straight from Toronto. The house was humming, with Ruth Chapman firmly in command, ordering this here and that there, inspecting everything, making lists and sending the lists back to town on the steamer.

But she hadn't said that she wanted Ben there on Saturday. Maybe she didn't realize that she hadn't told him. Maybe she just assumed he knew. He'd been waiting all week, with growing confusion. This was going to be a party unlike anything anyone up here had seen before. There were now thirty-four confirmed guests. Almost all of them would be staying at the Muskoka Beach Inn, a resort at the south end of the lake. The *Cherokee* had been chartered to ferry the guests from the inn to the cottage and back. A few of the guests were cottagers themselves, from the islands on Millionaires' Row, up the lake.

"And did you hear?" Jane Miller, one of the women who had been hired to help clean the cottage, told him that morning. "The Earl of Bessborough is coming."

"Who's the Earl of Bessborough?" Ben asked.

"The governor general!" She looked at him in surprise. Ben had some idea of what a governor general was: a British lord, or some such, who lived in Canada and signed papers in the name of the king.

"The governor general and Lady Bessborough are coming down in the Eatons' yacht from Port Carling and staying right here overnight," Jane Miller explained. "Can you imagine having an earl in your spare bedroom?"

"No wonder she wants us to change the sheets," Ben joked. But now he really, really wanted to be at the party. Maybe she'd want him to play his violin. Maybe the governor general square danced.

It was late Friday afternoon, and he had nothing particular to do. A cook had arrived, a thin man with a thick mustache, and taken over the kitchen. Dinner would be beef Wellington, which was even fancier than stew, apparently. Mostly the cook was getting everything ready for the next day, but he had ordered everyone out of the kitchen, and the cottage was as ship-shape as it was possible for a cottage to get, so Ben had pretty much run out of jobs. Ruth Chapman obviously thought so, too.

"Thank you, Ben, for everything."

"Sure." But still she hadn't said anything about tomorrow. He had to know. Maybe, if he suggested it. It was agony to push himself forward, but he was desperate.

"Um …" he looked down at his feet. "Is there anything that I could do for you, maybe, tomorrow?"

She looked at him a bit vacantly. "Tomorrow?" Then she realized. "Oh, no, no. I have people coming in from Toronto."

"Oh." He should have realized. This was a real party, a fancy affair. He had no place there.

"I thought maybe I could play you a square dance." He tried to grin, to make it sound like he was joking.

She smiled. "That might have been fun, actually. But we're going to have to make do with a string quartet. And I don't think there will be any dancing."

"Oh … okay. Well … have a good party."

"Thank you." She seemed ready to say something else for a second, but then she turned away, and he turned away and went down to the dock and rowed back to the Landing, which now he knew for sure he would never leave.

He prayed for rain, out of spite, but the day was gloriously sunny and warm, and not even humid. He tried to ignore the water taxi — the *Mildred*, out of Bracebridge, could hold up to forty in a pinch —

docking every few hours, though eventually the pull of curiosity dragged him down to the dock, where he invented work for himself and watched the busyness across the way. First it was just the cook, in white, with a tall hat, and two assistants and more boxes. The next trip it was half a dozen men and women, and yet more bunches of flowers. The men wore black suits with white shirts, and the women wore black dresses with white trim. Then came four others, in white tie and tails, carrying musical instruments. The string quartet, which was the worst thing of all. Real musicians, with real violins, playing real music. And he could have been there, listening to it. Just that, nothing else, would have been enough. If she had just let him sit in the kitchen and listen. She must have known how much that would have meant to him.

The dock, the kiss. He'd thought she was telling him that she understood, that she knew what he was going through.

But she'd just had too much to drink.

At four o'clock, the *Cherokee* arrived at the island with a couple of dozen people, casually elegant, the men in light-colored suits, the women in summer dresses, everyone delightfully amused to be in such a charming, rustic environment. Ruth Chapman was there at the dock to greet them, along with two waiters carrying trays with glasses of what Ben knew was champagne because he had hauled up the cases.

Over the next hour, boats arrived, bearing more guests. Ben couldn't understand why the boats tied up next to one another, all on one side of the dock, until the reason appeared at five, when the yacht arrived: a small steamer, maybe forty feet long with an ornate wooden cabin lined with windows perched on its deck, gliding sedately to the free side of the dock. A couple emerged, and Ruth Chapman curtsied, which meant the guy must be the governor general. Ben couldn't make out much from the distance. A middle-aged man in a white suit, a woman in a yellow dress. Who cares? Ben glowered to himself, loitering around the side of the house so Ruth Chapman wouldn't see him if she looked over. It was no big deal. Who was the governor general anyway? It wasn't like he was *real* royalty or anything.

Ben and his mother and Henry ate dinner in silence and after dinner they sat outside for awhile, until it was dark, not talking much, and then his mom went to her room to read — romance novels, the same ones, over and over — and Henry went to his to sleep, and Ben went to his to lie on his back, staring at the ceiling. The evening breeze brought snatches of string music and a faint hum of conversation and women's laughter. He imagined them sitting at that long table, the trees rustling, the lanterns lightening the dark, the candles, the flowers, the assistants gliding about, removing this plate, filling this glass, the violins in the night air, and Ruth Chapman, at the end of the table, in a beautiful blue dress, watching everyone and guiding the conversation and smoking discreetly. Or are you allowed to smoke around a governor general?

He wanted to be there so badly. Even if he wasn't playing the fiddle, even if Ruth Chapman didn't introduce him to anyone, even if he was just one of the waiters and nobody knew his name, just to be there, to see these people, to watch them eat and drink and listen to their conversation, these people who were so much more aware of the world than anyone in Muskoka, who said daring things and laughed at what they said, and were clever and knew it, and enjoyed it. He wanted to be there so badly.

He got off the bed and went downstairs quietly, and outside, down to the dock. There was a moon — of course there would be; it was a perfect evening; Ruth Chapman had ordered one — glinting silvery off the lapping water. He could see the lights of the cottage filtering through the trees, and the lanterns. Dinner was over, the music was a bit livelier: "How'd You Like to Spoon with Me?" He knew it. Were they going to dance after all?

He had to. He didn't know why. He just had to. He kicked off his shoes, slipped off his clothes and dove into the water.

Total dark. It was always disorienting to dive into water at night. Which way was up? But his head soon broke the surface. The water was calm and warm. He stroked steadily away from the Landing toward the island, through the dark water.

It took ten minutes, maybe less. His hand touched wood, and he pulled himself half out of the lake, blinking the water from his eyes.

The lanterns lit the staircase up to the cottage, and the cottage itself was vivid with light. There were people in the clearing in front of the cottage, in the cottage, silhouettes, voices, snatches of conversation.

"But really, I couldn't have, could I?"

"We knew them from Cairo, actually."

A woman stepped onto the veranda and walked to the end. It was her; he was sure of it. And then she lit a cigarette, and he was really sure. She was alone, surrounded by all these people, listening to the music drifting from inside, smoking her cigarette, thinking. Of what? What was she thinking all the time? And why wouldn't she think of him? Why hadn't she asked him to help? He would have done it for free. He wanted to be up there so badly.

A man came out and walked toward her. Her age, perhaps — it was hard to tell. He handed her a drink and said something to her, and she laughed, and he touched her elbow, and she turned to go back inside, and then looked down toward the dock.

He was farther out of the water than he'd thought, and there was a lantern on the tree at the foot of the dock. Could she see him? He slipped back into the water, hid behind the dock, then peered cautiously around it.

She was looking down at the dock. Had she seen him? Oh God, what if she'd seen him? If she came down, if she realized. Oh God.

The man said something to her. For a moment she continued to look down at the dock, then turned away and went back inside.

The swim back was longer. The energy had gone out of him. What had he been *thinking*? Had she seen him? What would she think? Maybe she hadn't seen him. Maybe it was too dark. Why in God's name had he gone over there? How much farther was it? He was tired. What had he been *thinking*?

Finally, home. He heaved himself out of the water, shook himself, ran his hand through his hair to get the water out, grabbed for his pants, pulled them on, groped for his shoes. He looked up. A shadow against the darkness. Henry was there, watching him. Ben looked down, shivering in shame.

"You don't belong over there," Henry said.

Anger rushed through him. He jerked his head up, defiant, furious.

"*WHY NOT?*" He had never yelled at Henry before in his life.

"Because you're better than they are."

And Henry turned and walked away.

Fall

The heat broke, finally, the week after Labor Day. Now there was a nip in the air at night, and the sky was dry and royal blue, reflected in choppy water freshened by a finally clean breeze. It was always a fine time, the first hint of fall, the first night for a blanket, but it was also a warning. The hard months were approaching.

Many of the visitors to the lake left on Labor Day weekend, but Ruth Chapman wasn't in a rush. He would see her sometimes, out on the dock, a sweater wrapped around her, reading a book. Nights were starting to come earlier, and the music from the Victrola drifted across the water earlier, and her lights went out earlier.

It was the middle of the month. Ben and Henry had been over to Browning Island to fix a leaky roof reported by a departing cottager. When they got back, Ben's mom told them at dinner, breaking the routine silence.

"Mrs. Chapman was by. She's leaving tomorrow.

She wants Ben to go over first thing. Three dollars, same as before."

Ben nodded, trying to pretend he was more interested in the meatloaf on his plate. He didn't want to go over there. He was ashamed. What if she had seen him? And even if she hadn't, he didn't want to go over there. He was ashamed.

But three dollars a day was two dollars more than anyone else on the lake was paying for help with closing up a cottage. He was there early, only to find there wasn't much to do. She had packed her things, including the booze, what little was left of it. The china was in crates, and the silver, and the bed sheets, and the towels and, well, pretty much everything. He'd thought she'd be leaving more behind. No one was going to disturb the cottage over the winter.

"Good morning." She came into the living room carrying a hamper of food — flour and sugar and tea and things. "I'd be grateful if you'd take this back to the Landing. There's no point shipping it all the way to New York."

He sensed it in her, too: a certain awkwardness, almost embarrassment. It seemed strange; she'd always been so confident. It only made things worse.

"You want me to start putting sheets over things?" he asked. The sheets would keep the dust off, and the mice.

"No." She shook her head. "Everything's going.

There should be a steamer along any minute. I've hired some men to help. But you can give me a hand with the shutters."

She was leaving for good. One summer at Pine Island. That was it. She hadn't liked the place, the lake, the island. She didn't want to come back. They swung the shutters closed on each window and latched them, one by one. It was the strangest feeling. He had fixed the hinge on this shutter, sanded and painted it. It had meant a lot to him. It was as though he owned the place a bit, had put himself into it. But for her, what was it for her? One summer, and then she got bored. Of everything. Of him.

They were at the icehouse. He tossed the blocks outside to melt in the autumn sun while she swept the sawdust. While she was sweeping she began to talk, not looking at him.

"It was a wonderful summer. I needed to be away from everything, and I was. It was what I needed after ... last spring. Just to be alone for awhile. But I'm not the sort of person who sits around. Next summer I want to travel. Europe, probably. I haven't seen France in years. Maybe I'll sell this place. I don't know. I might come back. But not next summer."

"Oh, okay."

Okay is what you say when you don't have anything to say.

A baritone whistle warned of the *Segwun's* approach.

Ben went down to the dock as the steamer sidled up. There was Cal, and there were half a dozen other men, and no one else, because there were few passengers on the ships this late in the season and Ruth Chapman had paid to ensure that her retreat from the lake was the *Segwun's* main task for the day.

The piano they had struggled to haul up to the cottage they struggled to haul back down to the dock. And the leather sofas and the heavy beds and the dressers. Everything they had sweated over in June they sweated over again now, and even the September breeze didn't keep Ben's shirt from soaking through.

"So, how's it going with Elsie?" Ben asked Cal as they staggered beneath the weight of a cedar chest filled with books.

"Ah, we broke up on Labor Day," he huffed in response. Fall was fatal to romance. "You should come into town some time. We could catch up."

"Yeah. Or you could come out here. We could go bass fishing."

"Hey, that's an idea. Maybe we could get my brother to sneak us a couple beers."

"Nah, I'm never gonna drink again."

"What happened?"

"Tell you about it later."

"Not even one?"

"Well, maybe just one."

It was mid-afternoon before they had everything

squared away. Ruth Chapman was at the dock, poring over a list.

"So, if you could take the boat back to Greavette's, they'll put it in storage. And if you can keep an eye on the cottage, say, once a week, here's a key. And here's my address and phone number in New York. Call collect. And here are some post-dated checks. I'll send you more. I may rent the place out next season, in which case we'll need to make some arrangement …"

Ben nodded and said, "Sure" and "Okay." Finally, she ran out of list. She paused.

"Well, that's it then."

"Okay."

"Thank you for all your help this summer." She smiled. "I enjoyed our conversations."

He could feel the blush. "So did I."

She was carrying a parcel wrapped in brown paper and tied with string.

"I have a present for you." She handed it to him. "You can open it when you get back to the Landing."

"Oh … you don't need to —"

"I know someone who knows someone who plays the violin. These are pieces he says you should be studying. You should pay special attention to the Bach."

Ben found it hard to speak at the best of times. The present left him far short of speech.

"And there's a card in there," she added. "It has

the name of a man who teaches violin at the Royal Conservatory of Music in Toronto. Apparently he's very good. I've sent him a note about you. If you ever get to Toronto, you should look him up."

"Oh." He couldn't think of anything to say. He couldn't even think of "thank you."

She held out her hand. He shook it. She clasped her other hand around his.

"You know, I never had a son," she said. "And I had no idea, before, how sorry I am about that." She reached forward and kissed him quickly on the forehead, then let go of his hand.

"Good-bye, Ben."

She walked smartly up the ramp and onto the boat. Ben helped Cal raise and secure the ramp. Cal was looking hard at Ben, eyes wide. Ben said nothing.

He said nothing as the boat steamed away, and nothing when he got back to the Landing, but went straight to his room and opened the package, took out his violin and started to play.

Cal showed up a week later, and they spent practically two whole days in the punt — up at dawn to fish for pickerel, then trolling along the shoreline for pike, or parked off a weed bed casting for bass. The cooling waters were good for pickerel especially, and Ben's mother appreciated the sweet-tasting fillets,

which she fried up for dinner the first night and
lunch the second day.

Cal did most of the talking because that was Cal,
and Ben enjoyed listening to him going on about
the perils and pleasures of having a girlfriend, and
his hopes of turning part-time work at the hardware
store into something more permanent, and the
prospects for bagging a deer or maybe even a
moose this year. It was near the end of the second
day, when they were sitting in the mouth of the
Muskoka River letting their hooks rest on the
bottom, hoping the minnows would attract one last
school of pickerel on their way to dinner, as the
sun lowered in the sky and a cool breeze ruffled the
lake, before Ben finally brought up the only thing
he could think about anymore.

"Cal, you ever wonder?"

"Wonder what?"

"I dunno. What we're gonna do?"

"You mean like jobs?"

"Yeah."

"I told you, I'm hoping Clipsham's hires me full
time."

"And that's it?"

"I dunno, what else is there?"

"I dunno."

They sat silent for a bit, then Cal spoke.

"You figure you're gonna stay at the Landing?"

Pause. "I guess so."

"You don't have to, you know."

Ben looked up quickly. "What else is there?"

"I dunno. You could always move into town. Maybe we could get a place. I'm sure ready to stop living at home."

Ben shook his head. "They need me at the Landing. Besides …"

"Besides what?"

"Don't you ever … I don't know." Big breath. "Don't you ever think of getting out of here?"

The question startled Cal. "You mean like move away?"

"Yeah."

Cal reeled in his line to check his minnow, and to think. "I don't think I'd wanna do that. I mean, I wish I was back on the lake, but the town's not so bad." He looked at Ben. "You thinking of leaving?"

Ben hunched his shoulders. "Probably not."

"Where'd you go?"

"I dunno. Toronto, maybe."

"And do what?"

"I dunno. Play the violin." He would never have told that to another person in the world. He instantly wished he hadn't told it to Cal.

Cal frowned. "But that's not a job." Then he looked at Ben. "Oh. Well, why not?"

"It'll never happen."

"Who knows? It might."

"How?"

Cal had no answer. They went back to watching their lines, until Cal asked, quietly.

"You're not very happy, are you?"

Ben shook his head. "How can you tell?"

"I've known you since first grade."

"Yeah, well, I guess." Ben straightened up. "I just ... I just see everything that's gonna happen. I'm going to stay at the Landing, or move into town, and that's it. And, I dunno, I'd figured there'd be more."

"Yeah, well, you always were different, playing the violin and everything."

"Yeah, well, right now I wish I'd never started."

"You'd have just done something else. You're pretty strange, you know. I mean you read, even when you don't have to."

Ben laughed. He couldn't help it. "Anyway, sun's going down. We better head back." They started to reel in their lines.

"Hey, Ben ..."

"What?"

"I think you oughta just get out of here," Cal said, his voice low. "You oughta just go."

"I can't."

"I know. You oughta anyway."

"Thanks."

They secured their hooks, and Cal picked up the oars. Ben looked out for a moment across the lake. The sun was sliding behind the pines that lined the western shore, and the islands were turning to silhouettes in the approaching twilight as the water darkened to gray-blue and the waves lapped against the rocking boat.

"Though I don't know why anyone would want to leave this lake," Cal said.

"Yeah, I guess."

Cal dipped the oars in the water and turned the boat for home.

The *Waome*

The October day was darker than gray, with a cold rain and a sullen chop to the water, as the *Waome* steamed out of the Indian River into the north end of the lake. Ben and Henry had gone up on her the day before, to Lake Rosseau, to look over McCulloch House, a large, white, wooden, ramshackle resort that sprawled across McCulloch Island, in the middle of the lake. In its day it had been one of the finest addresses in the district, a place where men in white flannels played tennis on its four courts and women of a certain age protected themselves against the sun by sitting under umbrellas as they gazed out at the lake, or at the men in white flannels. But the McCulloch family had sold the resort in the twenties, because fashion had moved on, to resorts where tennis gave way to speedboats and jacket and tie wasn't required for dinner. The resort had closed down soon after the Depression started. But now John Hotchkiss had bought it, because John Hotchkiss made a living out of buying things and then selling them, or renting them out. He owned some shacks on the edge of

Gravenhurst that Ben's mom said she wouldn't let a dog sleep in, but men slept in them in the winter when they worked on the lakes cutting blocks of ice for the railroad, or in the summer doing odd jobs, until there were no odd jobs left to do and they moved on. John Hotchkiss had grown fat and happy off what he bought and sold, and he had one of the biggest, brickest houses in town, and now he owned McCulloch House. Ben and Henry had spent the day touring the place with him.

"Cut-rate weekends, family packages, that's the thing," Hotchkiss had explained. "Cut every expense, cut staff back to the bone, simple food, canoe rentals. Make Muskoka affordable to people who can't afford Muskoka."

The place was run down, and it would take work. Henry had walked through the property — the main building with its dining room and lounge on the main floor and rooms on the second floor with the bathroom down the hall; the outlying cabins clustered around and behind it — pointing out leaking roofs and rotting planks.

"It'll take six men three months to get it in shape," Henry predicted.

"How about four men and two months," Hotchkiss countered. "We only need to fix the worst of it, the parts you can see."

It was the parts you couldn't see that did in a house, Henry had often said. But he just scowled and agreed to take the job and to find two other men. This would mean work for both of them through April and May.

"I know you'll do fine," Hotchkiss smiled, as they shook hands. "I hear you and Ben did a bang-up job on Pine Island."

It was late when they were done, so they had spent the night at Port Carling — Hotchkiss paid for a room but not a meal, so dinner was the baloney sandwiches Ben's mom had made them and a cup of tea — and waited for the *Waome* to pick them up in the morning. By ten o'clock they were on their way back home.

Ben stood on the starboard railing, gazing down at the choppy water, the collar of his canvas coat pulled up, his wool hat jammed over his ears, and tried to ignore the rain. It was warmer in the cabin, but Henry was in the cabin, and he had had enough of Henry, who'd kept him awake the night before with his snoring. He'd be spending two months with Henry on that island, working on that lodge. They'd sleep there at night and cook their own food and maybe get off the island on weekends — or maybe not, if they fell behind on the work. In the weeks since Ruth Chapman had left the island he had felt as though the air had gotten heavier and harder to breath. He knew his mom sensed it.

"What's the matter?" she had asked him one day the week before as he turned the wheel that turned the blades that chopped the turnips his mother was feeding into the machine. The cows loved turnips, and the fattening pig would love turnips for a little while longer.

"Nothing," he'd replied, because what could he tell her? That he felt trapped, and she was part of the reason?

"Son." She straightened up and looked at him. "What's bothering you?"

"It's nothing."

"Ben—"

"I said it's nothing!" And he had stalked away and gone to his room and stayed there till dinner, which they ate in even greater silence than usual.

Something might happen, his mother had hoped. You never knew. But now he did know. Nothing happened.

The sheet music that Ruth Chapman had given him, it was all beautiful, but a lot of it he just couldn't play. There were too many notes, and he couldn't handle the fingering; he twisted his fingers in knots, it seemed, trying to figure out how it should be done. Patience, his mother had urged, as he stormed into the kitchen from the toolshed one morning, frustrated by music that seemed just out of reach. Patience and practice. But that wasn't it. There were things you had to know how to do, skills, techniques. Someone had to show you. There was no one here. He had taken the music into town once and shown it to Ambrose, who just shook his head. "Way beyond me. This isn't fiddle music. This is violin music. And we're just a couple of fiddlers, Ben. Though who knows, if we'd had a chance ..." He didn't finish the sentence, because he didn't have to.

There was one piece Ben had dedicated himself to. He practiced it day after day. It was called a chaconne, by Bach, for solo violin, and playing it chilled Ben, made him shiver. Most of it was slow, which at least made it playable, though in other places there were leaps and double-stops and scales that he knew were beyond him. But he had practiced it every day for a month, and he was starting to get some of it. The piece opened with a cry of despair — wailing notes of pain and loss that made Ben gasp the first time he played through them. Then came a melodic line, simple at first, but grave, severe. The melody built on itself, doubled back, sped up, turned into cascades of notes that Ben's fingers and brain were too thick to play, but he tried anyway, pushing himself through it. There was math in it, Ben could see, in the way the composer took different lines of melody and wove them together, intertwined them, then drew them apart. But the music always doubled back, returning to its roots: pain, loss, and then whatever comes after loss. What was it? Ben couldn't define it. An ache, but a memory, too, a remembrance, an acceptance. It was so beautiful, beautiful beyond crying. When they got home today, he'd practice some more after chores.

Henry was standing beside him. Ben hadn't heard him approach. He leaned over the railing, as Ben was leaning, and looked down at the water, as though he was trying to see what it was Ben was staring at. But Ben wasn't staring at anything.

"Hotchkiss doesn't pay one cent more than he has to." Henry's mouth twisted into a smirk. They weren't getting half what Ruth Chapman had paid, but it was the only work around, so they took it.

"Guess that's why he's rich and we're not," Ben joked, if it really was a joke.

"Guess so." They were silent for a bit, but Henry spoke up again, as though he actually wanted to talk, which was strange, because Henry never wanted to talk, unless it was to complain.

"But it'll be a change, anyway, working up there."

Ben couldn't be sure, but it almost seemed to him that Henry had been easier on him since the night on the dock. He wasn't riding Ben as hard about chores, and took more time to explain how things were done. "Yeah, I guess so," Ben agreed, though it wasn't a change he was looking forward to. "Anyway, it's not like we have a choice."

"Nope." Henry looked back down at the water. "We don't have a choice. We never do."

We never do. Ben let the breath out of his lungs, slowly. Henry knew it, too.

There was something strange about the water. It was even grayer, darker than before. Ben looked up.

"Henry." Henry caught the undercurrent of worried surprise in Ben's voice and straightened up.

"Jesus," he breathed. "Would you look at that."

They were in one of the widest parts of the lake, with two miles of open water to the west, leading into Bala Bay. A cloud was racing across that water beneath the overcast sky — dark, ugly rain sheeting down from it, the lake roiling underneath. Squalls were common on the lake — sudden gusts of wind and wave that came on you in a minute and lasted a few minutes and then moved on. You could usually see them coming, like you could see this one. The thing to do was to turn your bow into the wind and ride it out. But Ben had never seen a cloud like that, that big, that black, that fast. And the *Waome* wasn't turning.

Alvin Saulter, who was manning the engine and boiler room, came out on deck for some air. The crew outnumbered the passengers this late in the season. Besides Saulter there was a cook, a man to stoke the boiler, the purser, the mate and Bill Henshaw, the captain. Everyone knew Henshaw: he'd been sailing the ships of the Muskoka Navigation Company his whole adult life, and he had a reputation as a careful captain who could tell a good story. Apart from Ben and Henry, the only passenger was a Presbyterian minister on his way to Bracebridge — a polite, gentle man, who had retreated to the relative warmth of the dining room one deck below as soon as the boat cleared the river. The second smallest steamer in the fleet was the only one still plying the lakes, and now that the cottagers were all gone it mostly just carried supplies and mail. This would be the last week before the entire fleet went into winter quarters.

"That's a dirty looking piece of weather out there," Saulter muttered.

For a second nobody said anything as the squall approached. Then Ben realized. The storm was coming at them from the starboard stern. Captain Henshaw wouldn't be able to see it.

Henry realized it at the same instant.

"He's got to turn the boat." Henry was right beside the wheelhouse. He limped two steps and yanked open the wheelhouse door.

"Bill!" he yelled. "Turn 'er to —"

And then it struck.

Ben was hit by a moving wall of wind and water that sucked the breath out of his lungs and lifted him off his feet and flung him through the door of the cabin. He wasn't afraid — he was too astonished to be afraid. He had never felt anything like this — anything even *remotely* like this — in his life. A second later, the force of the blast drove him against the far wall of the cabin, and a terrible pain stabbed through his left shoulder and down his chest. The pain made him yell out. And now he was very afraid.

A second shock: water — numbing, cold, October water, flooding over him. This made no sense. He was in the cabin, two decks above the lake. Why was there water?

Nothing made sense. The wall of the cabin was beneath him, and water surged through the windows, and the floor he had been blown and skidded across was now a wall. Then he realized. The force of the blast had heeled the *Waome* over onto her port side, pushing the cabin walls and windows under water. Water was rushing through windows and doors, filling the cabin. The ship was in trouble.

The deck was almost perpendicular now. He was trapped. The only way out of there was the door that he had been blown through, the door on the other side of the cabin. Only now it was overhead, like a trapdoor, and there was no way to reach it.

Yes, there was. He was only a few steps from the wall separating the cabin from the wheelhouse. There was a small table bolted to it, and a fire ax. He could use them to climb.

The ship groaned, and there was a sudden crash overhead. Was it the funnel breaking loose? Were they in that much trouble? Then a new layer of fear gripped him. Water would be rushing into the boiler room. When it hit the red-hot metal of the boiler, the boiler could explode, blowing up the ship and everyone still on it.

Panic gripped him. He was going to drown. He was going to die. He had to get out.

Blindly, he thrashed toward the wall. The table was under water, but he could stand on its edge. He heaved himself up, then reached up and grabbed the fire ax with his left hand, wincing at the pain in his shoulder, and reached for the door with his right hand. It was too far. It was too far. It was too far and the boat was sinking and he was going to die. He wasn't thinking now. He bent his knees, then launched off the table, lunging for the edge of the doorway. Three fingers of his right hand grabbed it, clung to it, and with the strength that only comes with white terror, he pulled himself up, out of the water that was trying to suck him back down, until he could grab the edge with his other hand, and though pain coursed down his left arm he chin-upped his way out of there. He was still alive.

But he was outside on a ship heeled to port, alone. The wind raged at him, and white-capped waves smashed against the ship, which was almost completely on its side. She could roll over any second, trapping everyone beneath her hull. Except there wasn't anyone else. He couldn't see a soul. The railing he had been leaning over less than — my God, it hadn't been a minute ago — was now above him. He reached up, grabbed it for support and stood. How was he going to get out of here? He'd have to climb up on the railing and then slide down the side of the boat into the water. Then what? But there was no then. There was only this minute. Trying to live for one more minute.

And then, through the fog of the panic, he remembered. Henry.

He had been at the wheelhouse, yelling at Captain Henshaw. Except the wheelhouse was now almost completely under water. Where was Henry?

Keeping one firm hand on the railing, then another, Ben groped toward the wheelhouse. He was there in a matter of seconds, but there wasn't much to see except water beneath him and darkness, and — a hand! groping for the opening. Ben grabbed Henry's bony hand. It was white cold, clammy, and the grasp was weak.

"Henry!" Ben shouted over the wind. "Come on!"

But there was no response. Just the weak clasp. Something was awfully wrong.

Ben lowered himself into the water, gasping at the cold. It was dark. Everything was under water, the wheel, the engine signal, everything. Ben blinked the water out of his eyes, trying to orient himself.

"Ben?"

In the corner, in the thin pocket of air between water and wall, he could make out Henry's head, gasping, gulping, his left hand clinging to a window sill.

"Henry, we've got to get out of here!" Ben yelled. The wheelhouse could be under water any second.

"Can't swim." Ben knew that. Henry hadn't swum a stroke since the accident, decades before.

"I'll help you." Ben tried to get his left arm around Henry, tried to ignore the pain gripping his left side. He had no idea how he was going to lift him out of the wheelhouse, but he had to try.

But Henry pushed him away, or tried to. He was awfully weak.

"No. Go on."

"No!" Ben reached his arm around again, tried to pull Henry away. But he was clinging to that windowsill with every ounce of strength he had, which wasn't much.

And then everything began to shift again. Metal groaned, wood ripped and splintered and snapped, and for a terrifying moment Ben was sure the *Waome* was capsizing. But instead she was righting herself, floor becoming floor again; walls, walls.

Except they were still up to their chests in water, and as Ben watched, wide-eyed, the bow of the ship began to lift out of the water. The *Waome* was going down by the stern, and she was going down now.

Ben suddenly realized that Henry was clutching him, shivering. Ben turned to speak, but his words choked on the shock. Henry's head was matted in blood. He could see the gash, ugly, oozing blood, which started on his forehead and ran down almost to his right ear. He was shivering violently, his eyes unfocused, unthinking.

"Come on." Holding his uncle, Ben waded out of the wheelhouse, onto the sloping deck. The ship was sliding under and would take them with her if they couldn't swim free of the undertow. Ben propped Henry up against the railing, climbed onto it, and lifted Henry over. Pain shot through his elbow, and he cried out. But Henry was over the side and in the water, and so was Ben, surrounded by pieces of wood and rope and other debris from the ship. The *Waome* was slipping away beneath them, and Ben could feel the suction tugging at his legs. Flailing, he reached for a couple of pieces of wood and propped them under himself and Henry. It was enough. In a moment, the suction had stopped. The *Waome* was gone.

And now things were much, much worse. Four-foot waves with frothing caps washed over their heads, one after the other, driven on by the howl of a wind that seemed to push them as fast as a current. Ben's sodden clothes weighed him down, and his shoes were like anchors. He and Henry were holding onto two boards nailed together, a yard or so long, part of the deck, probably, but they weren't enough to keep both of them afloat, and Henry's head started to disappear beneath the water. Frantic, Ben let go, then used the toe of one shoe to kick off the other, and his own toes to pull off the other shoe, so at least his feet were free. Shrugging off his canvas coat, he pulled Henry as far onto the board as he dared before it started to sink again, then backed off. He could keep Henry's head above water, and one arm, but that was about all.

And Henry wasn't helping. His eyes were half-closed, his mouth half-open, and he barely sputtered when water washed over him. He let out a low moan.

"Henry!" Ben yelled. "Come on! We have to swim!" He wasn't sure if Henry even heard.

Where was land? Ben looked around, desperate, and panic started to seize him again. They were in open water, but there was an island maybe five hundred yards to the north. On a calm, warm day, an easy swim. Weighed down by clothes, weighed down by Henry, with four-foot waves, in October water, his left side throbbing, could he do it?

"Ben!"

The voice came over the water, to his right. It was Reg Leeder, one of the crew. He was bleeding, too, and clinging to a chair. Ben wasn't alone. His heart lifted.

"Make for the island!" Leeder shouted.

"No!" It was another voice. George Harvey, the purser, about ten feet away. "The wind's too strong. We have to swim with the wind." He pointed in the other direction. "That one!"

Oh my God.

He knew the island, Keewaydin. He'd delivered

some wood there a year ago, for the cottage on it. It was half a mile away. And already the water had numbed his fingers. There was no way.

"Come on," Harvey yelled. "Swim for it!"

Ben threw his left arm around Henry. "Let's go, Henry. Just hang onto the board. Let's go home."

He could see others in the water now. Alvin Saulter had made it out, and Bob Bonnis, a big man who had been tending the boiler, and there was Captain Henshaw.

"Come on, everyone!" Harvey yelled. "We swim or we die!" Ben kicked his feet and carved into the oncoming wave with his right arm. Kick. Stroke. Kick. Stroke. Live. Live.

"Where's the captain?" someone yelled. It had only been a couple of minutes, but already Ben's mind had started to shut down. He jerked his head up and looked around. He'd seen Captain Henshaw in the water just a few moments before. Where was he now?

"He's gone," Harvey yelled out. "He's gone."

He was in his sixties. Too old, the heart too weak, the water too cold. Ben looked at Henry. His head was rolling side to side. "Henry!" Ben yelled, trying to wake him. "Henry, come on, wake up!" Nothing.

He had to get Henry to shore. He had to get help. Ben fixed his eyes on the island, then lowered his head, and kicked and stroked. He had to get there. He had to.

The wind tore at him, the waves washed over him, the pain down his side throbbed and pierced. Before long, he wasn't thinking of anything, wasn't aware of anything. Kick, stroke. Kick, stroke. Get help. Get help.

"Ben." A hand touched his shoulder. George Harvey was beside him, treading water. He was a broad-shouldered man and a fine swimmer, and he was looking at Ben.

"You have to let go of Hank."

"What?" Ben jerked his head left, and gasped. Henry's eyes were open. A wave washed over them, but Henry didn't blink. His skin was gray-white, his mouth slack-jawed.

"Henry!" Ben grabbed his shoulder and shook him, treading water, ignoring the pain. "Henry, come on, wake up!"

"Ben!" Harvey grabbed him. "He's gone. Come on. He's gone. You can't help him. Let him go."

"No!" Ben cried. "Henry, come on! Wake up!"

Ben yelled, Harvey yelled, the wind screamed.

Then Ben stopped yelling. Henry hadn't heard any of it. The grip on the board was a death grip. He was dead. Henry was dead.

"Ben." George Harvey looked him in the eye. "You have to swim." He let go of Ben's arm, and then started to swim away, looking back. "Come on."

Henry's right arm was floating in the water. Ben draped it over the wooden board. He wouldn't leave Henry without the board. He wouldn't do that.

"Henry ..."Ben was sobbing."I'm sorry. I'm sorry."

"Ben!" Harvey was already twenty feet away. "Come ON!"

"I'm sorry." Ben let go of the board. The next wave pushed Henry away from him. The next wave pushed him farther still. "I'm sorry." Then he turned away and began to swim. But he didn't know if he even wanted to live.

Henry. I'm so sorry. Forgive me.

It was easier, for awhile. He could use both arms, and he wasn't trying to pull another body along with him. He looked up after a couple of minutes, and the island seemed a little bit closer. Before, every time he'd looked, it had almost seemed farther away.

But pain coursed up and down his left arm, and it was weak, unable to plough as strongly through the waves. And his wool pants and heavy flannel shirt weighed him down, and the chill water had already numbed his toes and fingers, and the numbness was spreading deeper.

"Come on, everyone, we're halfway there!" Harvey shouted to the others.

"We'll make it, you'll see!" Saulter shouted back.

"Damn right we will!" Bob Bonnis yelled. Ben said nothing. He hurt. He was tired. He was numb.

Stroke, kick. Stroke, kick. *I'm sorry. I'm so sorry.*

Every few minutes, someone would yell in encouragement, and others would yell back. Ben stopped listening. He focused on the pain of his left arm, on the waves washing over him, on the black blur ahead. Minutes passed, tens of minutes. He was so tired, so tired.

"Come on, Ben! You can do it!"

"Swim for it, Ben!"

"You'll make it, Ben!"

Ben looked up. He had fallen behind the others, maybe thirty feet or more. They were looking back, yelling at him, trying to encourage him.

"Come on, son, you can do it!"

"Swim for it, Ben!"

But his arm hurt, and he was tired. And Henry was back there. He had left Henry.

"Come on, we're almost there!"

Ben stopped swimming, squinted, rubbed the water off his face. The island was closer. Not a blur anymore, but pines and rocks you could see. George Harvey, leading the pack, was maybe only a couple of hundred yards from shore.

"Don't give up, Ben!"

"Swim for it!"

The swim to Pine Island wasn't any longer. It would be like swimming over to her dock. He was tired. But he wanted to live. Yes, he wanted to live.

He started swimming again, head down, forcing his left arm to work, refusing to give in to the pain, kicking his heels, turning his face to the side, grabbing air, then plunging it under water, then turning to the other side, grabbing air. He was swimming so slowly, so slowly. But he wanted to live. He wanted to live. Come on, you swim or you die. Breathe, breathe. It hurts. I'm so tired. Come on, come on …

"Come on! Come on!"

He looked up. The rocks were in front of him, maybe ten yards out. The other men were already on shore. George Harvey was holding the branch of a birch tree out over the water.

"You're here. Just a little farther. Come on!"

He yelled out loud, in anger, in defiance, and stroked toward the branch, so close, now closer, even closer … Yes!

He was pulled toward the rocks, and then arms grabbed his shoulders. He cried out in pain, but the others ignored the cry and heaved him out, and suddenly he was on land, curled up, shivering.

"Hang on, Ben. Bob's breaking into the cottage. We'll get a fire going."

Ben knew there was a stove in there. He'd delivered the wood.

The others left him, made their way toward the cabin inside the woods. Ben didn't move. He sat huddled, his knees under his chin, looking out over the gray waves, searching for a head above water, a miracle, something, somehow.

There was nothing there.

Finally, the others came back for him and carried him inside.

Chaconne

Snow fell on the slate-gray water, and a sheen of ice crept out from shore. Ben shivered. It was cold, too cold to be going out on the lake. But this would be the last time.

His mother had gone back to the house, leaving him alone on the dock. She was delaying, trying to think of excuses not to leave.

"I'll just have one more look around," she had said before walking back up the hill. "To see if we've missed anything."

But she had already had a dozen looks-around and more. There was nothing left. Their clothes, two pots, two pans, a few knives and forks and the like, a few pictures, an old kerosene lamp that his mother refused to part with were packed into two trunks that the two of them had lugged down to the launch, which would take them on one last trip into town. They would leave the boat at Greavette's and take the train to Toronto, and then — well, neither of them knew exactly what would happen after that.

It had taken an hour before people realized that the *Waome* was so overdue that something had to be wrong, and another hour before a boat from Beaumaris reached the island, where the men — drier, thanks to a fire, but still in shock and disbelief — clambered in and huddled together, for the trip across a lake that was calm again. Ben wanted to go straight back to the Landing, but they were all taken instead to the little hospital in Bracebridge, where they were poked and prodded and someone put the kettle on for tea. The doctor, a fussy man, or so it seemed to Ben, put Ben's arm in a sling and taped his chest — he'd bruised some ribs and pulled something in his shoulder; he wasn't really listening. He sat in the corner, numb, saying nothing whenever someone came over to offer comfort and say they were sorry for his loss. It was mid-afternoon before his mother arrived — the Schultzes had a phone and had gone over in their old launch to tell her the news and take her to Bracebridge. When Ben saw his mother, he said nothing, stared at her, mute. Henry was dead. Her brother. It was his fault. He had tried, but not enough. It was his fault. She should blame him. He had failed Henry, failed her. But she looked at him for one moment, and then folded him into her arms, and he began to cry, and she was crying, and people left them alone.

The men found Henry's body the next day, and they buried him the day after, the same day they buried Captain Henshaw and the minister and Art Thompson, the mate, who had been trapped with the minister inside the ship, where they drowned. The sinking was front-page news for a day, and then everyone moved on, leaving Ben and his mother alone at the Landing, with winter closing in. The night of the funeral his mother had told him that she had decided to sell the Landing. Ben had stared at her, amazed.

"Sell?"

"We couldn't keep it up, even if we wanted to, and we don't want to."

Ben didn't want to, he'd never wanted to. But it was different for his mother.

"This is your place."

She shook her head.

"I left this place once and had to come back. This time I'm not coming back."

John Hotchkiss bought the Landing, for less than it was worth, of course. But that was the Hotchkiss way. He had money when others didn't, and could make an offer when people just had to sell. Anyway, they both just wanted to get away from the place.

But there would be enough for them to live on for awhile in Toronto, and that's where they were going. "I'll find work," his mother promised, "and you'll find work, and you'll take music lessons."

"We can't afford it." Ben shook his head.

"Yes, we can." She reached her arm across the table where they were sitting, a kerosene lamp the only light in the kitchen, and took his hand in hers. Before he would have flinched, and pulled away. Not now.

"You need to learn to play the violin as well as you can," she told him. "That's what matters now. So that's what we're going to do."

Ben smiled. "And that's all there is to it?"

She smiled back. "You're learning."

He had written to the professor that Ruth Chapman had told him about and had received a reply within a week, telling him to call when he reached Toronto to arrange an audition. His mother had been right after all. If you made yourself available, things happened. Ruth Chapman had changed his life in ways he still hadn't worked through. But now he would be in Toronto, living in some basement apartment, probably, working all day at some job he hated, but playing his violin for real now, taking lessons from a real teacher and — and what? Who knew? Things were going in directions he had never expected them to go. It was frightening, and thrilling. And he had a New York widow who smoked two packs a day while drinking a bottle of gin and who swore and laughed and played him Sibelius and taught him how to pour wine to thank for it. He had so much to thank her for. Even if she had broken his heart, just a little.

He'd sent the checks she had given him to the address she had given him, with a note explaining what had happened. That was two weeks ago, but there'd been no reply. Maybe she was in Europe or something. Or maybe the lake had become the past for her, too.

Ben watched the snow falling on the water. Last night he'd woken up again, sweating, Henry's lifeless face staring at him from his dreams. In a way, he accepted what the others were telling him, what his mother told him over and over: that Henry couldn't swim, that he had lost too much blood from the cut on his head, that Ben had done everything he could, more than most men could have done, that it wasn't his fault. Sure. But Henry was in his dreams at night and tugged at his thoughts through the day. The lake, the Landing, they were in Henry's bones, they were his life. The Landing for Henry was like the violin for Ben. But Henry could never love the thing he was chained to, hated the truth of it, hated the truth that he could never leave it the way Ben and his mother were leaving it. They were abandoning the Landing the way Ben had abandoned Henry, Ben thought to himself. Henry would never have left the Landing. Would he have left Ben on the lake?

Ben only knew that he missed Henry, missed him every day, and wanted him back.

His mother was still up at the house, trying to let go. Ben lifted the case that rested on top of one of the trunks, took out the violin and the bow, rested the violin on his shoulder up against his chin, tuned a couple of strings and began to play the chaconne, letting its long, slow, keening notes drift on the wind, through the snow over the gray November waters of his lake.

Historical Note

On October 6, 1934, late in the morning, the steamship *Waome* was struck by a sudden storm on Lake Muskoka, north of Toronto. The ship sank in less than a minute. There were three fatalities: Captain Bill Henshaw, Arthur Thompson, who was serving as mate, and the Reverend L.D.S. Coxon, a passenger.

A Note from the Author

My goal in writing *The Landing* was to craft a book that was faithful to the place where I grew up, and to the generation that raised my generation. To the extent that this work of fiction also tells a true story, others deserve much of the credit.

My mother, Phyllis Ibbitson, nee Boyd, grew up on a Muskoka farm during the Depression and learned to play the piano the way Ben learned to play the fiddle. I asked her countless questions, some ridiculously detailed, and she answered them all. Thanks, Mom.

I used to work for Jim Groh when I was in high school; in the decades since, we have been good friends. Jim grew up not far from where Ben grew up, and was able to fill in numerous gaps. Doug Chamberlain, whom I've known longer than almost anyone outside my own family, knows everything there is to know about cottage repair, including the rebuilding of stone steps. His father, Doug, Sr., allowed himself to be peppered with questions during a couple of fishing trips. Thanks to all of you, my friends.

Cyril and Marion Fry, Shirley Barlow and Cecil Porter are all dedicated to preserving and promoting the history of Gravenhurst and Muskoka. They read the manuscript, offering many valued suggestions for improvements and correcting dozens of minor historical errors. I am very grateful to them.

The people of Muskoka love to talk about their past, and write about it, too. I owe debts to the authors of *The Light of Other Days; Gravenhurst: An Album of Memories and Mysteries; The Years Gone By: A History of Walker's Point and Barlochan, Muskoka, 1870–1970; Through the Narrows on Lake Muskoka; Browning Island, Lake Muskoka: Cottagers Remember the Good Old Days; A Legacy Almost Gone: An Anthology of Kilworthy Country,* among others. Many of these are privately published reminiscences compiled by dedicated but anonymous authors. They and others like them offer an invaluable record of the life of the district's pioneers.

I owe an enormous debt to Richard Tatley. Not only did he write *The Steamboat Era in the Muskokas* (Erin, Ont.: Boston Mills, 1983–4, 2 vols.), but he also read my manuscript and corrected numerous errors. I also owe him an apology. When the *Waome* was struck by the storm, Richard observed, Ben could not have fallen into the lounge, as there was no door to the lounge on the starboard side of the ship. But that had to happen, for narrative purposes. So I invented a door, and also rearranged the location of people on the ship to put Ben in the lounge, alone. I know Richard understands, but I also know that this meticulous historian will regret such inaccuracies.

Alex Kehler is both an accomplished violinist and fine folk fiddler. His enthusiasm for the story, and his suggestions on making the passages about violin playing more accurate, helped enormously. After reading the manuscript, he says, he pulled out the complete Bach sonatas and partitas for solo violin and began playing through them, "as best I can."

I have been trying to write a book about Muskoka my whole life. In 2001, in a midtown Manhattan bar, of all places, I worked out this story. But it was harder to write than to imagine; I tried several times to get it down, but the words just wouldn't come. Finally, my agent, John Pearce, suggested I sit down and craft the most detailed outline I could. I did, and suddenly the book became possible. I owe you, John.

Sheila Barry, editor-in-chief of Kids Can Press, read that outline and immediately offered to publish the book and to edit it herself. Three drafts later, I can honestly say that there is not one sentence I could make better. That's what the very best editors do. I am also grateful to Margaret Allen for her meticulous copy edit.

Finally and foremost, Grant Burke lived through the writing of this book and put up with its obsessed author, for which the author is, as for so many other things, deeply grateful.

All of these people came together to help make this story better than it would have been without them. Anything that is false or wrong is my doing.

There is one additional bit of artistic licence in *The Landing*. Jasha Heifitz's landmark recording of the Sibelius violin concerto was released in 1935, a year after our story takes place. But I let Ben hear it anyway.

Washington, D.C.
November 11, 2007